"Has anyone ever told you that playing hard to get doesn't work if a man loves to chase?"

"Who says I'm playing hard to get? You couldn't get me even if you tried." Normally, their banter went back and forth like this for hours, but today his silence caught her off guard. She turned toward him and placed her hands on her hips.

"What's wrong, Walker? Cat got your tongue?" She would have said more, but the mischievous look in his eyes told her to stop while she was ahead.

"I can think of a lot of things I want to do with my tongue, and each and every one of those things would bring you the utmost satisfaction."

She couldn't help the hitch in her voice at his accusation. Apparently, she wasn't thinking as quickly on her feet as she normally did. He glanced behind her before curling his hand around her waist and pulling her into a corner of the hallway. He leaned his forehead on hers in a way he never had before. The endearing gesture only made her breathing more staggered.

Dear Reader,

I couldn't wait to get my hands on Jaleen Walker and Danni Allison!

You initially met Jaleen in my first novel (wow!), *A Tempting Proposal*, from my Elite Events series. Jaleen is better known as the jokester playboy and loyal sidekick. You met observant and feisty Danni Allison in *Enticing Winter* and have been able to get to know her throughout the Bare Sophistication series.

Surprisingly, I tried to pair Jaleen with several heroines in the Elite Events series, but it never felt right. When I decided to write the Bare Sophistication series, I immediately knew that Danni was his perfect match. Although both characters appear to have it all figured out, that couldn't be further from the truth.

I received numerous emails and messages asking for Jaleen and Danni's story, so I'm extremely excited for you all to join them on their journey!

Much love,

Sherelle

authorsherellegreen@gmail.com
@SherelleGreen

Nights of Fantasy

Sherelle Green

HARLEQUIN® KIMANI™ ROMANCE

Recycling programs
for this product may
not exist in your area.

ISBN-13: 978-0-373-86494-2

Nights of Fantasy

Copyright © 2017 by Sherelle Green

For questions and comments about the quality of this book please contact us at CustomerService@Harlequin.com.

H HARLEQUIN®
™ www.Harlequin.com

Printed in U.S.A.

Sherelle Green is a Chicago native with a dynamic imagination and a passion for reading and writing. She enjoys composing emotionally driven stories that are steamy, edgy and touch on real-life issues. Her overall goal is to create relatable and fierce heroines who are flawed just like the strong and sexy heroes who fight so hard to win their hearts. There's no such thing as a perfect person…but when you find that person who is perfect for you, the possibilities are endless. Nothing satisfies her more than writing stories filled with compelling love affairs, multifaceted characters and intriguing relationships.

Books by Sherelle Green

Harlequin Kimani Romance

A Tempting Proposal
If Only for Tonight
Red Velvet Kisses
Beautiful Surrender
Enticing Winter
Wrapped in Red with Nana Malone
Falling for Autumn
Waiting for Summer
Nights of Fantasy

To my parents, Mary and Carl,
for always being my rocks and biggest supporters. Words
can't express how extremely grateful I am to have you both
as parents. Even as a young girl, I knew my parents were
special. Now I can't help but admire you even more. You
are the two most selfless people I know, and if it were in
my power to do so, I'd give you the world! You are both
role models to so many and you give so much to others
without ever asking for anything in return. When I think
about you both and try to find the words to explain you
to others, the first adjective that constantly comes to mind
is…*exceptional*. You're exceptional individuals and the
most hardworking people I know. Thank you for your
unconditional love and encouragement.

Acknowledgments

To two people who mean the world to me—my sister,
Nikki, and husband, Henry. There are times when
you can't control the factors that stand in the way of a
deadline. Throughout writing this book, you both were
my saving grace. Thank you for the endless conversations,
awesome brainstorming sessions and words of
encouragement. I'm not sure I could have completed this
story without your love and support.

Prologue

Six months ago…

"If you want me to leave with you, you'll have to kiss me first."

Jaleen Walker glanced at his friends before setting his eyes on the woman who was making it extremely difficult to keep his distance. He'd arrived at the bar ten minutes prior, along with the other men celebrating his friend Aiden's bachelor party.

When Aiden Chase had received a call from his soon-to-be wife, Summer Dupree, Jaleen'd watched Aiden's face turn from excitement to concern when he learned his fiancée had had one too many fruity drinks. It had only taken a minute for Aiden to announce that he wanted to crash Summer's bachelorette party.

Since Summer was like a little sister to Jaleen, he hadn't argued with Aiden and had quickly informed the guys that the bachelor party was about to become coed. Jaleen hadn't even known Aiden for an entire year, but the two had immediately hit it off when Summer had taken him to a holiday celebration last year.

Summer and Aiden were getting married in less than

forty-eight hours and Jaleen couldn't be happier for the both of them. It seemed like all of his friends were tying the knot and he'd been to more pre- and postwedding celebrations over the past few years than he could count.

Now that the men had arrived at the chic Miami lounge, they learned that Summer wasn't the only one tipsy. Most of the women appeared to be feeling a buzz and dancing as if they didn't have to get up in the morning for rehearsal. Reacting quickly, each husband, fiancé or boyfriend went to their significant other to join them on the dance floor, leaving only those unattached to watch the scene unfold.

"I'll be right back," Jaleen said to Danni, ignoring the way her lips curled into the perfect pout.

Jaleen looked at the remaining men and motioned for them to group together. "Maybe we should get all the women some water," he suggested to his friend Luke, Aiden's friend Dax, Summer's cousin Malakai and a few others. "Then I'll ask Aiden and the others if they need help getting any of the other ladies back to the hotel. But, fellas, let's remember that these women are friends with Aiden and Summer, so we have to act respectfully."

"Agreed," Dax said as the other men nodded their heads. "I think I have a bottle of aspirin in my rental car, so I'll grab that, too."

Jaleen glanced at Malakai, both men knowing that the statement was made for the men who weren't either family or like family to the happy couple. They didn't have to worry about Luke and Dax because both were stand-up men.

Once they'd gotten the bottles of water and aspirin ready for the women, they returned to the group. Jaleen almost laughed at the way Luke and Dax made a beeline for two of Summer's friends and business associates, Nicole LeBlanc and Aaliyah Bai.

"They are so predictable," Malakai said, shaking his head. "I assume you're going to find Danni?"

Jaleen didn't have to respond because Malakai was already heading over to the other men to assist with a couple of Summer's high school friends. It was well-known news that although Jaleen and Danni were constantly bickering, they had a close friendship. He wouldn't be surprised if bets were going around the group that they'd be the next pair to start dating. But Jaleen knew that could never happen. He wasn't exactly a one-woman type of man. Although he never dated more than one woman at the same time, he had a reputation for not allowing a woman to make it past the one-month mark.

Jaleen glanced around the VIP area and dance floor, finally finding Danni in the corner of the lounge. As he approached, he tried to ignore the soft sway of her hips as she moved to the beat of the music. *She looks beautiful.* All the women were wearing teal dresses while Summer was in all white. Despite the fact that the dresses were each similar in style, it was Danni's teal formfitting dress that had his undivided attention.

"There you are," he said when he'd reached her. "Why are you all the way over here?"

"Because I knew you would find me." Her eyes sparkled with interest. "And I didn't want all our friends to see when you kissed me."

Jaleen ran a hand down his face. *She's not going to make this easy.* He couldn't even remember how long he'd waited to finally feel how soft Danni's lips were. However, he wanted her to be fully conscious of her decisions when he kissed her. She wasn't sober, which meant he had to keep his lips to himself.

He glanced down at the glass she was holding. "Danni, I don't think you mean that," he said, reaching for her drink. "How about we trade this drink out for a bottled water?" She accepted the water and took a nice long sip. He tried not to watch the way her lips curled around the bottle, but he failed.

"I do mean it," Danni said as she closed the distance. "The only way I'm leaving this bar is if you kiss me like I've seen you kiss so many other women."

Jaleen winced at the comment despite how true it was. "I do want to kiss you, but how about I kiss you tomorrow night instead?"

She tilted her head as if trying to decide if she could trust to him or not. "Hmm, okay, that might work. As long as you actually kiss me so that I can mark you off my list."

Jaleen raised one eyebrow. "And what list might that be?"

"My special list that I made on my birthday," she said with a cheesy grin. "My 'Thirty Things To Do Before I'm Thirty' list."

Jaleen did a quick mental calculation. She'd just had a birthday, so he assumed she hadn't gotten far on the list.

"You're on it more than once," she said in almost a whisper.

When she ran her fingers down the collar of his shirt, he made no effort to stop her. *A special list.* It sounded like a bucket list of sorts and he knew Danni was big on lists. She was the only woman he knew who didn't just make a grocery or chores list, but rather a list to remind her she'd created a list for groceries and chores. He often teased her about being overprepared, but she denied it each and every time.

She rested one hand on his chest, moving her fingers in a small, circular motion. Her touch was innocent, but his thoughts definitely weren't.

"I think we need to get you back to the hotel," he said

as he searched for their friends. He noticed that the others in their group seemed to be preparing to leave, as well.

"Did the ladies drive?" Jaleen asked Aiden as he approached him and Summer.

"No, we had a driver," Danni answered instead. "But I sent him away since I figured we could walk back."

The hotel wasn't that far from the lounge, but tugging along ten tipsy women wearing heels seemed like too much work.

"Let's head back," Aiden said with a whistle as he twirled a finger in the air. The group started filing out of the lounge toward the parking lot. Aiden, Summer and Danni hopped into Jaleen's car while everyone else divided into the other four cars.

"I want to sit with Summer," Danni said as she pulled Summer to the back of the car, leaving Aiden to sit in the front with Jaleen.

"Well, this isn't exactly how I thought your bachelor party would end," Jaleen said with a laugh as he pulled out of the parking lot.

"Tonight with you and the guys was a lot of fun." Aiden glanced back at Summer. "But the fact that I get to spend the rest of the night making sure that beauty in the backseat doesn't have a hangover isn't a bad way to end the night, either."

The amount of love Jaleen heard in Aiden's voice didn't surprise him. If anything, it made him envious that he'd never get a chance to experience the type of love Aiden and Summer shared. His eyes caught Danni's in the rearview mirror. *What is it about Danni Allison?* For years he'd wondered why the only woman who seemed to be immune to his charm was the same woman who was constantly on his mind.

He supposed that's the reason they'd developed an actual friendship. Although he still teased her any chance he got, he was well aware that Danni knew entirely too much about his dating history and, for that reason alone, he couldn't even get her to agree to go on one date.

After they arrived at the hotel and parked the cars, Aiden and Summer bid good-night to the group. The ladies all boarded the elevator a couple minutes later to head to their rooms, while the men went to the bar in the hotel lobby.

Jaleen had just sat at the bar when Luke nodded his head toward the front of the lobby. Jaleen followed his gaze.

Danni was standing near the hotel entrance with her clutch in her hand.

I could have sworn she just got on the elevator.

Jaleen turned back to Luke. "I'll be right back."

"Yeah, right," Luke said with a laugh as he turned to the other men.

Jaleen caught Danni's arm as soon as she took one step outside the door. "Where are you going?"

"To get something to eat."

Seriously! "It's almost three in the morning. Nothing is open."

"Well, I'll find a gas station, then. They never close." She took one more step out the door.

"They have twenty-four-hour room service," Jaleen said, stopping her again. "How about you order some food in your room?"

A sly smile crept onto her face. "On one condition."

He was almost afraid to ask. "What's that?"

"You come to my room and eat with me."

Jaleen groaned. "If I do, will you eat and then get some rest before tomorrow's rehearsal?"

"Yes," she said a little too quickly. Before he knew it, Danni was tugging his arm and leading him toward the elevators.

The second they arrived at her hotel room, Danni tossed her clutch on the table and kicked off one heel. When she went to remove the other heel, she stumbled.

"Whoa, pretty lady," Jaleen said as he helped her steady. "Let's be careful."

"I'm tired of being careful," Danni replied, looking him in the eye before turning her back to him. "Can you unzip my dress?"

No, I can't unzip your dress. "Sure," he said instead. He felt like his fingers were moving in slow motion as he worked the zipper to reveal the back of a sexy, white-and-teal lace bra. It would take little effort to unclasp the sole clip, but he wouldn't dare do that tonight.

"There you go," he said, allowing one sole finger to run down her spine. She gasped at the touch before turning around to face him.

"Are you sure you won't kiss me tonight?" She looked so vulnerable standing there and something in her eyes made him want to say to hell with what he'd said earlier and take a sample of what she was offering. Luckily, his brain was thinking more than the other part of his anatomy.

"Not tonight. But if you ask me tomorrow, you'll get a different answer."

For a minute he thought she was going to ignore what he was saying, but instead she walked to the couch to lie down.

"How about I order that room service?" He walked over to the desk. "What do you want?"

"You decide," she said, curling onto her side. "I just need something to eat."

The last thought he had before he ordered was that the best food they could both have right now would be if they feasted on each other.

Sunlight seeping through the curtains caused Danni to awaken. She glanced at the clock on the nightstand—*8:00 a.m.* She checked her iPhone, surprised that she hadn't set her alarm. As a matter of fact, part of the night was a blur. She'd planned on waking up a little earlier to meet a couple of the bridesmaids for breakfast before rehearsal in a couple of hours.

Maybe I can still meet them, she thought as she stretched her body. It was then that she noticed she was still wearing her dress from last night. *What the...?* The back of her dress was unzipped and one shoulder was out of the strap. Her hands flew to her mouth as memories of the previous night came rushing back to her.

Jaleen was here. He came back to my hotel room with me. She also suspected he was responsible for the glass of water and aspirin on her nightstand because she didn't recall getting it herself.

She got out of bed, grabbed a sundress and her toiletries and made her way to the bathroom. A shower would definitely wake her up and, hopefully, help her remember more details. Thirty minutes later she was showered, dressed and no closer to remembering all the details.

When she walked back into the bedroom, a pair of shoes in the corner of the room caught her eye. *Those are Jaleen's.* Although she couldn't recall if he was wearing them last night, she'd seen them on him before. *Why exactly did I see Jaleen last night?* They'd been celebrating Summer's bachelorette party while the men had been out celebrating Aiden's bachelor party. She didn't know how they'd gotten together last night, but she vaguely recalled asking Jaleen if he would kiss her.

Oh, God. I did ask him to kiss me. She couldn't think of anything more embarrassing...except if he was still in her suite somewhere. She opened the bedroom door and tiptoed around the corner to the living room area. As suspected, Jaleen was sprawled out on the couch with his long legs hanging over the side. She'd always found him attractive— although she'd never admit that to him—however, the sight before her nearly stole her breath.

He still had on his jeans, but he'd discarded his socks and unbuttoned his shirt, exposing his washboard abs and deep vee of his hip bone now causing her imagination to wander to places it never had before. *That's a lie.* She'd definitely spent more time than she would ever admit wondering just how sexy Jaleen Walker would look naked. Of course, she'd never go there with a man like him... A man that seemed to trade out women as quickly as he changed underwear. However, there was no harm in admiring him while he slept.

Even in his sleep, his jawline was well-defined and she'd bet that he'd just gotten his goatee freshly cut and hair lined yesterday before the bachelor party. How many times had she wanted to run her tongue across his smooth, cinnamon-brown complexion? As cocky as he was, Danni was surprised there was anything about him she found attractive. He was not her usual type. But lately she'd been looking at him in a way that she knew she shouldn't but couldn't help.

She froze when he slightly adjusted himself on the couch, noticing for the first time just how close she actually was to him. She took a step back when his hand reached out and lightly grabbed her wrist.

"Not so fast," Jaleen said groggily. "How do you feel?"

She momentarily couldn't find the words to respond as

she stared into his deep brown eyes. "I feel okay," she finally said. "Thanks for taking care of me last night."

"No problem," he said, sitting up on the couch. "I only stayed to make sure you were okay."

Her eyes briefly left his to stare at his lips. *What has gotten into me?* She was usually a lot better at getting a handle on her attraction to Jaleen. Maybe it was being with him all alone in her suite that had her feeling bold? Or maybe it was the fact that she'd had a long couple of months and giving in to temptation sounded like a good stress reliever.

"Did I ask you to kiss me last night?" she asked.

His eyes darkened. "I'll be right back," he said as he made his way to the bathroom.

She blinked her eyes in confusion at the sudden movement. Unsure of what to do with herself until he returned, she sat on the couch and tried not to breathe in his masculine scent that still lingered in the room.

When he returned, he looked a lot more put together than she felt. "So did I ask you to kiss me last night?" she repeated.

"Maybe a few times." He sat next to her on the couch. "But I knew you were tipsy."

She was almost afraid to ask, but had to. "Why didn't you kiss me?"

His lips curled to the side in a smile. "Trust me, I wanted to. But under the circumstances, it didn't feel right."

"Because I was too tipsy."

"Something like that," he said with a laugh. "The first time we kiss, I want you to be completely alert about what's going on."

Her cheeks grew warm and her heartbeat quickened. She was sure she'd regret what she was about to say next. "What about now?" Her voice got slightly lower. "I'm completely alert now."

Jaleen gave her a look of confusion as he studied her eyes. She knew why he was confused. Up until now she'd done everything she could to try to deny their obvious chemistry. But this was a new year and she was a new Danni. This year, she planned to face her fears unlike she had before. Even so, the longer they sat there staring at one another, the more she regretted her decision to say something in the first place.

"You know what? Never mind. I'm not sure what's gotten into me…" Her voice trailed off as Jaleen's face got closer to hers.

"There's no chance I'm ignoring what you said." Jaleen's hand lightly grazed her cheek. "I've waited too long to see how soft your lips are."

She held her breath as his lips inched closer to hers. The somersaults in her stomach only increased when she felt his breath mingle with hers.

"Now would be the time to stop me," Jaleen said as a warning. Danni didn't have any intention to stop Jaleen but unfortunately the loud knock on the door did.

"Danni, are you in there? We have to meet the ladies for breakfast."

Jaleen dropped his hand and Danni sighed at the sound of her friend's voice. Hearing Nicole was like a jolt to her senses.

"Maybe you should go," she said, standing from the couch.

A hint of disappointment flashed across his face before he stood, as well. "I guess you're right."

They made their way to the door. "Do you want me to stay here until you leave with Nicole?"

"That would be great," she said with a nod. "I'd really appreciate it." She grabbed her clutch and quickly exited her hotel room before she dwelled on what had almost happened between her and Jaleen.

It wasn't that she thought kissing him would be a bad thing. Her fear was that kissing Jaleen would be the best thing she'd experienced in a long time.

Chapter 1

"Sorry I'm late," Danni said as she rushed into Bare Sophistication Boutique and Studio minutes before close. "I ran into some traffic on my drive from Tampa to Miami."

"No worries. How is your mom?" Summer asked as she finished ringing up the last customer.

"She's doing well! She's looking forward to the day when she'll have all three of her children in the same place at the same time."

"Does that mean your brothers haven't visited in a while?"

"They've visited, but I've told you stories about how random their visits are. Dominic is still overseas, but we're hoping he'll get a leave soon. And Aaron is off chasing whatever his next adventure is. I swear, between the two of them, I can barely keep track of their schedules."

"I can't wait to meet your mom," Summer said as she locked the front door of the shop and flipped over the open sign. "She seems like the type of mom I always wanted to have."

Danni didn't miss the sadness in her voice. It was no secret that Summer's mom, Sonia Dupree, was as far from a motherly figure as you could get. Danni could still recall the horrible stories she'd heard from Summer and her older sisters, Winter and Autumn, about their mother.

Sometimes, Danni still worried that Sonia Dupree had affected her daughters in irreversible ways. However, all three Dupree sisters were married to wonderful men. Winter was married to Taheim Reed. Autumn was married to Taheim's brother, Ajay Reed. And Summer and Aiden had been doing wonderfully ever since they tied the knot. All three couples were proving that true love existed and could happen when you least expected it.

"She's looking forward to meeting you, too," Danni said. "I told her I'd bring you down for a mini vacation one day."

"Speaking of vacations, have you talked to Jaleen lately?"

"Um, no. Why do you ask?"

Summer straightened a few lingerie pieces on the rack. "No reason. Just wondering if you finally returned his calls."

Ever since they'd almost kissed in the hotel room before Summer and Aiden's wedding, Danni had been making a conscious effort to avoid Jaleen at any mutual parties they attended. Avoiding him had been easy since he lived in Chicago and she now lived in Miami. However, for the past four months Jaleen had been handling some work in Europe for his family's real-estate business overseas and, for some reason, he'd been hell-bent on emailing, texting or calling her any chance he got.

At first she'd enjoyed communicating with Jaleen since they had, indeed, been friends for years. Yet the closer it got for him to return to the States, the less she returned his calls, texts or emails. He probably assumed that he'd done something wrong, when, in actuality, she was the person pushing him away. She had a good reason, but she doubted he would understand. Honestly, she doubted any of her friends would understand.

"Okay, I'm all set," Summer said as she turned off the lights. "Are you ready to head to dinner?"

Danni froze. "You mean we're still on for dinner?"

"Of course we are! Tonight we're celebrating the fact that you are almost done with your master's in fashion merchandising. Going back to school and working full-time is a huge deal. Especially since our Bare Sophistication store in Miami has only been open a little over a year. So we definitely have to celebrate. Nicole, Aaliyah and Aiden should already be at the restaurant."

At least she didn't mention what I thought she would.

In two months she'd be finished with her degree, which meant she would have to officially accept the partnership Summer and her sisters had offered her during the grand opening of the Miami store.

When they'd initially asked her to be a partner of the Bare Sophistication chain, Danni had been overcome with emotion considering the Dupree sisters had always dreamed of being in business together and Danni had just joined the team as store manager for both the Chicago and Miami locations. She'd never dreamed they'd give her such a huge opportunity. Her celebration was short-lived when she'd realized that despite how wonderful the opportunity was, she still had a major dilemma standing in her way of officially accepting the offer.

"Yeah, I'll trail you in my car since I don't want to leave it here overnight," Danni said. Her iPhone rang just as Summer was locking up the store. She shuffled through her purse to try to catch the call.

Definitely not answering that.

"Who was it?"

"No one," she said as she stuffed the phone back in her purse.

"Hmm, are you sure it wasn't a certain friend of ours who's been contacting you for months?"

"I'm not sure who you mean." She took out her car keys as they made their way to the parking lot.

"You know exactly who I'm talking about, even if you don't want to tell me what happened during my wedding—"

"Nothing happened," she interrupted.

"Well, regardless of what did or didn't happen, I think you should call him back. I just spoke with him a couple of days ago and he said you're avoiding him. I've never known Jaleen to even care if a woman avoids him."

Danni hated to admit that she was equally curious as to why he'd been reaching out to her these past few months. Yeah, they'd had a special moment in her hotel suite the day before Summer and Aiden's wedding, but she didn't see how that equated to him contacting her so much.

"Okay, fine. I'll call him back after dinner."

"Or maybe you should call him before dinner," Summer suggested before getting into her car.

"Or maybe I'll just keep avoiding him unless I head to Chicago for the semiannual sale Winter and Autumn are having at the Bare Sophistication Chicago location," Danni said under her breath as she got into her car, as well.

Danni had enough on her plate and that didn't include worrying about a certain handsome friend who just so happened to be the only guy she'd been thinking about for the past six months. *Or try the past few years.* It didn't matter if she thought about him a lot or a little. She shouldn't be thinking about him at all.

Maybe I should call him since I'll have an excuse to get off the phone once I arrive at the restaurant for dinner. That way, he couldn't convince her to stay on the phone any longer than five minutes since the restaurant was so close to the shop. She clicked the audio recognition feature of her car and called Jaleen.

He answered on the third ring. "Hey, beautiful."

She momentarily soaked in the warmth in his voice. He'd always called her *beautiful*, but lately she was starting to believe he really meant it.

"Hey, Jaleen. Just a heads up, I have to meet the gang for dinner so I only have five minutes."

"Duly noted," he said with a laugh.

"How are you?"

"Much better now that you've finally called me back. What's the deal? Screening my calls and messages?"

"Um, something like that. Why? Not used to women being so dismissive of your charm?" she said with a laugh.

"Not women who threw themselves at me one day then avoided me the next."

"I did not avoid you. I had merely been fulfilling my bridesmaid's duties. Besides, you haven't even been in the States for the past four months."

"Exactly. And we've been talking a lot while I was away, then you suddenly go cold turkey."

"Aw, did I hurt your little feelings?" she said with a laugh.

Jaleen was silent for about five seconds.

"Let's get one thing straight, Danni. There is nothing on me that is little, small, tiny or any other word used to describe the men you've been with in the past."

Her breath caught. "That's not what I meant and you know it. I was referring to you, not your male anatomy."

"Whether you meant to or not, you just offered me a challenge. And you know there isn't anything I love more than a challenge."

She didn't like the direction their conversation was

heading. "Anyway, I have to go. I just arrived at the restaurant, so I'll have to call you later."

"Will you actually call me later?" he asked. She thought about all the times she'd avoided his calls recently, knowing she had no reason to justify ignoring him. At least, no reason she wanted to explain to him.

"Yes, I'll call you later."

"Great. Then I'll talk to you soon."

She hung up the phone, parked her car and then leaned her head back on her headrest. *What is it about that man that has me so intrigued?*

She'd dated her fair share of men in the past… Even some that reminded her a little of Jaleen. Yet he got under her skin and the more she thought about it, the more she was unsure if that was a good or bad thing. By the time she stepped out of the car, she was already beginning to regret her decision.

"At least he lives in Chicago," she said as she reached to open the door to the restaurant.

"Let me guess," someone said, catching the door ahead of her and holding it open. "You're talking about me."

Danni dropped her arm instantly and her eyes widened in surprise. "Ja-Jaleen! What are you…how are you…what are you doing here?" *Oh, my goodness, am I stuttering? I never falter over my words.*

"It's nice to see you, too, beautiful." His eyes sparkled with amusement, but she was having a difficult time finding anything funny about the situation.

Man, he looks good. True, it had been a while since she'd seen him in person, but they'd FaceTimed a couple of times. Tonight he looked extra sexy in his dark gray jeans and collared blue shirt that was unbuttoned to reveal his white tee. His gray-and-blue Nikes only added to his look.

She'd never understood why, even in his casual clothing, he looked as if he were headed to a photo shoot.

When she finally made her way back to his eyes, he was smiling too hard for her liking.

"What are you doing here?" she asked again, walking through the restaurant door.

"I think a better question would be why didn't I mention I was in Miami when we were on the phone a few minutes ago," he said, following her into the restaurant. When she gave her name to the hostess, it dawned on her that one of their mutual friends must have mentioned the dinner to him.

"Who told you? Summer? Aiden?"

He shrugged. "Does it really matter?"

"You know I hate surprises," she whispered as they neared the table where their friends were waiting.

"And you know that had you answered my calls earlier, you would have known I was in Miami."

"I had good reason."

"And what reason would that be?"

She tried to ignore how close he was to her ear when he whispered. His scent was already filling her nostrils to a less than comfortable level. "It's a reason I'd rather not share right now."

"Fine. Have it your way."

They arrived at the table and greeted their friends. She was well aware that Summer's, Nicole's and Aaliyah's eyes were all on her as she sat, with Jaleen sitting right across from her.

"Are you okay?" Nicole whispered. Instead of responding right away, Danni took a large sip of water, hoping to cool off from the hot stares Jaleen was already shooting her way.

Danni, originally born in Miami, had attended two

years of high school with Nicole before Danni's family had moved to Tampa. The two had kept in contact and, when Summer had moved to Miami, Danni had reached out to Nicole to meet up with Summer. The two had hit it off immediately and later met Aaliyah, who was one of the lead photographers at a beauty trade show a couple weeks after.

When Danni had arrived in Miami to help Summer open Bare Sophistication, the four women had immediately bonded and later agreed to go into business together. They were still building the Bare Sophistication Miami empire, but with Nicole as the lead makeup artist and hairstylist for their boudoir studio, Aaliyah as the boudoir beauty photographer and Summer and Danni running the lingerie boutique, things were looking promising for the group of friends.

"I'm not sure," Danni finally whispered back. "Why do I get a feeling that I've just stepped into a bad horror movie?"

"That's a bit extreme," Nicole said with a laugh. "Jaleen is hardly a villain. You've known him for years."

"Why is he here in Miami? I have a few theories… One, he wanted to catch me off guard with his presence. Mission accomplished. Two, he manipulated his way into my celebration dinner by contacting one of you to get the details. Once again, well done on his part. And three, he is being very cocky and suspicious. Do you see how he's looking at me over his glass every time he takes a sip of water? All of those are characteristics of a villain."

"I think you're being a bit dramatic. Yes, he is all of those things, but I'm not sure that Jaleen's sole purpose is to make you uncomfortable. I agree that he probably wants to spend some time with you, but you both have gotten pretty close these past few months. Even if it was long-distance."

Danni stole another glance at him before turning back

to Nicole. "I'm telling you, something is off about him tonight. He's definitely up to no good."

"Maybe you need to experience his type of no good," Nicole said as she raised both her eyebrows. "Could be good for you."

Danni was about to respond when Aiden began talking.

"Jaleen, I meant to ask. How long are you staying in Miami? You're here for a business meeting, right?"

So he's here for work. How hard would it have been for him to tell me that? "At least he's only here for a meeting," Danni whispered to Nicole.

"Actually, I just had my first of several meetings here in Miami this morning."

Danni felt like she was holding her breath as she waited for him to continue. After another minute, she couldn't wait any longer.

"So how long will you be in Miami?" she asked.

He glanced around at everyone sitting at the table before his eyes landed on Danni. "I'll be in Miami for at least the next three months...possibly longer."

She studied his eyes for any sign that he was joking and realized he wasn't. "You're serious?" she asked because she had to for her own sanity.

"Dead serious," he said, not even breaking into a smirk as he held her gaze.

"I take back what I said," Nicole whispered in her ear. "Maybe you did just step into your own horror movie because if he's the villain, you're definitely his main target."

Danni shivered at the thought.

Not sure if that's a good or bad thing.

When he winked, she looked away and focused on the others in the group. Hard to do since her mind was on the man sitting across from her.

I'm screwed.

Chapter 2

Jaleen would be lying to himself if he said he didn't get a kick out of watching Danni squirm. In his defense, he'd tried to tell her about the contract he'd won in South Beach for weeks, but she hadn't returned his phone calls. Once he'd realized that she was ignoring him, he'd reached out to Aiden and Summer to try to figure out why she was avoiding him.

Twenty minutes into dinner and she still hadn't made eye contact with him again. Not that he could blame her. It was impossible not to feel the chemistry between them, despite how many months had passed since they'd last seen each other.

"I want to make a toast," Summer said, raising her wineglass in the air. "To Danni, who has almost completed her master's." Everyone clinked glasses and offered their congrats.

"And a second toast that may be a bit premature but long overdue," Summer continued. "Although my sisters couldn't be here tonight, on behalf of myself, Winter and Autumn, we'd like to express our gratitude and excitement to Danni, who will soon be the newest partner of the Bare Sophistication enterprise."

This time, even more congrats and cheers were offered, but Jaleen noticed that Danni's smile didn't quite reach her eyes. *That's strange.* As hard as Danni worked, he'd expected her to look a little more excited about the offer. He'd noticed her initial excitement over a year ago when the Dupree sisters had made her the partnership offer after the grand opening of their Miami store. It may have made sense to the others that she said she wanted to wait until she finished her master's—especially considering Summer, Winter and Autumn each had several degrees in the fashion industry—but it hadn't made much sense to Jaleen.

"Thanks so much, guys," Danni said as she took a sip of her wine. "I'm really excited to begin this new journey with the enterprise."

"We couldn't think of a more deserving person than you to be our partner," Summer said, briefly standing from the table to give Danni a hug.

Jaleen watched the embrace, thinking for the first time tonight Danni's response seemed genuine. Which further begged him to wonder why Danni was so tense regarding tonight's dinner topics.

Man, who are you kidding? You're probably the reason she's so tense tonight.

After dinner ended and they were making their way to their cars, Jaleen took a moment to pull Danni aside.

"Can we talk for a minute?"

She looked at their friends, who had just made it to the parking lot. "Sure. What do you want to talk about?"

Jaleen glanced down the block in the opposite direction. "Come walk with me."

She crossed her arms over her chest. "Is that your way of asking me to take a walk with you? Because it sounded more like a demand."

He smiled at her defensive stance. This was the Danni

he knew. The Danni who'd spent the past few years arguing with everything he'd said. Although he liked making her nervous, he liked her even more when she was fired up.

Tonight she had on a simple white tee tucked into a pair of high-waisted jeans. He may have loved to see her in dresses, but the woman could wear a pair of jeans unlike any other woman he knew. His eyes traveled farther down her body until they landed on her French-tipped toenails and peep-toe fringed boots. The outfit was perfect for the cooler seventy-degree March night.

When his eyes traveled back to her face, he admired the large brown curls adorning her smooth mahogany face and round dark ginger eyes. Despite all of her features that drove him crazy with desire if he allowed himself to think about her too long, it was her lips that always kept his gaze a little longer than they should. He'd never seen lips so rich and pouty, which was saying a lot because he'd seen his fair share of lips. Today her lips were decorated in a striking burgundy lipstick. A shade that only made him want to kiss her even more than usual. After a few seconds, her lips parted, causing him to take a step closer.

"How about we take that walk?" she said, placing a hand on his chest. He glanced down at her hand, trying to shake the visions of her lips softly kissing his body.

Once they began walking and he felt like he had a handle on his thoughts, he started the conversation.

"I wanted to apologize for surprising you by popping up in Miami. I suppose I could have left you a voice mail when you didn't answer."

"Yes, you could have," she said with a laugh. "But I should have returned your calls. Sorry about that."

"It's no big deal. Although I'm curious why you've been avoiding me."

She glanced at him before looking forward. "I'm sure

you already know why, but in hindsight, I guess I've been acting childish. I'm a grown woman avoiding a sexy man all because we almost kissed. Seems pretty pathetic when you say it out loud."

So she thinks I'm sexy? She probably hadn't meant to say it out loud, but it didn't stop him from enjoying the fact that she'd said it anyway.

"I guess I understand. But I thought that talking as much as we have these past four months while I was in Europe would have made you feel more at ease. I, for one, enjoyed our conversations."

"I did, too," she said, lightly touching his arm. Even though her touch was light, he still felt her warmth travel throughout his body. "I just have a lot going on right now and I'm afraid that you're a distraction I can't afford."

"I never asked you for anything other than friendship."

Danni gave him a look of disbelief. "Oh, come on, Jaleen. You and I both know that you don't do friendships with the opposite sex."

"We've been friends for years, right? Or do you deny it?"

"Yeah, but most of that time was spent arguing with one another. And I'm not sure if *friends* is the right word. *Close associates* may be more accurate since the only reason we communicated with each other was the fact that we shared so many mutual friends."

He wanted to tell her that he suspected they knew each other more than she gave them credit for, but he knew when to leave the battle to fight another day.

"Tell you what. While I'm in Miami, how about we work on building a friendship?" *That way, I can prove to you that it may be time to take this friendship to another level.*

She shot him a look of skepticism before her lips curled

into a smile. "Why do I have a feeling that you have an even bigger plan brewing in your mind?"

"I don't know what you mean." He feigned a look of innocence. "I'm just a guy asking a girl if she'll embark on a new friendship journey with me."

Danni rapidly blinked her eyes in surprise before she burst out in laughter. Soon, he was laughing right along with her. When their laughing began to die down, Danni spoke first.

"I'm curious as to what this friendship journey will entail and, although I want to say no, I'm too curious not to say yes."

"Good decision," he said as they walked in a comfortable stride. Jaleen really didn't have a plan brewing like Danni had assumed. But now that she'd put the idea in his mind, a friendship plan with Danni was exactly what he would concoct.

As Jaleen glanced around the poor excuse for a rooftop terrace of the South Beach boutique hotel he'd be renovating over the course of the next few months, he couldn't help but feel overwhelmed at the task before him. It was one of five hotels he had to flip and though he usually didn't stress out over jobs, he was stressing over this one.

Although the family business his grandfather had started began as a small real-estate company, Jaleen's father and uncle had grown Walker Realty Partner into a multimillion-dollar company. In the Walker family, your path was laid out for you from the time you were born. Both of Jaleen's older brothers each had a key role in the business, and although flipping real estate was a huge part of their company, Jaleen's specialty was flipping boutique resorts. It was something he'd started doing just to see if he could prove to his father that he could be an asset to the family business. Jael Walker was not a man who was easily impressed. Especially when he felt as though his youngest son wasn't cutthroat enough to make the decisions needed to get far in the industry.

"Hey, boss, where do you want us to start?"

Jaleen glanced over at Jesse, the head of his construction team. "Rally up the team in the back of the restaurant on the lower level."

"Will do."

When his father had informed him that their company had won the bid for five boutique hotels scattered throughout the heart of South Beach, the only reason Jaleen had been willing to return to the States after being in Europe was the fact that he'd known Danni was in Miami. Yeah, it was nice to know he had other friends there, as well, but he'd promised himself he'd live at least a year in Europe working out of the small international Walker Realty Partner office. Considering that his cousin was currently managing all of their international projects, it had taken more than a little persuasion for his dad and uncle to agree to a one-year hiatus from their projects in the States. His dad hadn't really agreed to the entire year, but his uncle's blessing had been enough.

However, little had he known how much was riding on the success of his South Beach renovations. To say that his dad and uncle had made some poor business decisions over the years was putting it mildly. Now, not only did Jaleen have the responsibility of getting this job done in record time, but his family's company was relying on the money they would get when they resold the properties.

"Okay, men," he said when he arrived at the restaurant. "Ideally, we'd love to finish this project in three months." A couple expected groans echoed throughout the room. "I know it's a tight timeline, but we've had tighter and managed to complete the renovation on time. On behalf of Walker Realty Partner, I'd like to thank each of you for all the hard work you continuously put into our renovations." Jaleen touched on a few additional key points before releasing the men to get started.

At the end of an entire twelve-hour day, he wasn't as confident that they'd make the deadline. He was almost to the apartment he'd rented for the duration of his stay when his cell phone rang.

"Hey, Aiden. What's up man?"

"Jay, I know it's last minute, but Summer and I figured we'd have a few folks over tonight for some food and drinks. We wanted to extend an invite to you if you're free."

Damn. He was so exhausted he couldn't even guarantee he wouldn't fall asleep sitting on Summer and Aiden's couch.

"I don't know, man. I'm pretty wiped out."

"Okay, so I'll be honest," Aiden said. "Summer is always inviting the ladies over and, usually, I either hang with them or I leave to hang out with some of the guys I've met since moving to Miami. But I called a couple of my guys and they are busy."

"So I'm your next best choice? I'm offended," Jaleen said, mocking irritation.

"Nah, man. You only just told us you'd be here for a while a couple of days ago, so it slipped my mind."

"I'm just messing with you." Jaleen ran his hand down his face as he weighed his options. "Is Danni going to be there?"

Aiden laughed. "Yeah, she'll be here."

"Then I'll see you around eight." He ended the call, excited that he'd finally get a chance to see Danni again. His excitement was short-lived when another call came in shortly after.

"Hey, Jeremiah. What's up?" Jaleen opened the door to his apartment.

"What's up, little brother? I hope you have an explanation for blowing off your meeting with Mr. Rose while you were in Europe. JW is furious."

Growing up, Jaleen knew that Jael Walker had never wanted to be called "Dad." Therefore his sons called him JW, as did most of his business associates. "Yeah, well, I was pretty upset when I learned JW had informed Mr. Rose that I would meet with him without clearing it with me."

"You know how Dad is. He always makes decisions without consulting us, which means you also know how important that meeting was."

"Well, things come up. I'll reschedule with Mr. Rose when I have the time." The line grew silent. Once Jeremiah got quiet, the conversation was either over for the time being or a second round of lectures would soon follow.

"If that's all you called for, then I need to get in the shower. Give the kids and your wife my love."

"Jay, before you hang up, can you promise me one thing?"

"It depends on what it is." He knew he was giving his brother a hard time, but he couldn't help it. Jeremiah and his other brother, Joel, always listened to what JW said. Half the time, Jaleen spent their serious discussions trying to decipher how his brothers really felt versus what their father had encouraged them to say.

"Can you promise me that after you turn thirty-five, you'll finally try to live your life the best way you can and stop all this foolishness? Everyone has responsibilities and although I know that it's difficult for you to accept some of yours, I also know you well enough to realize you'll eventually do the right thing. I'm not saying families like ours are normal, but we can't change what we were born into, so the easiest way to accept your future is to obey the rules and enjoy it as much as you can."

Jaleen let his brother's words sink in. He'd heard them one too many times before and, just like all the other conversations he'd had with Jeremiah, they always ended with him doing what was expected of him rather than what he actually wanted to do.

"I understand what you're saying, Jeremiah, and, as always, I appreciate the advice." Jaleen turned on the faucet for his shower. "And, as always, I'm going to remind you that I have six months until I turn thirty-five and, until then, I don't have to obey every command JW gives me."

"I know, Jay… I know."

They spoke for a couple more minutes about his niece, nephew and sister-in-law before disconnecting. He wasn't one of those types of people that didn't appreciate his blessings, but for once, Jaleen wished he didn't have several people moving around the pieces of his life as if he were a pawn in a chess game.

Stepping into the shower, he did what came natural every time he was reminded that his clock was ticking down and life got overwhelming.

He thought about Danni Allison.

Chapter 3

"Who's that at the door?" Danni asked Summer for a third time. Just like the previous two times, Summer simply shrugged as she continued to play their card game.

"Babe, are you going to get that?" Summer yelled to Aiden. Tonight, Summer and Aiden's beach home was the host location for one of their random Spades games. Danni and Summer were teamed against Nicole and Aaliyah, and they were tied one round to one round. They'd been playing Spades for an hour and, up until now, Danni's focus had been completely on winning the next round to win the overall game.

That all changed when the doorbell rang and she noticed the women share a knowing look. She wouldn't have cared that they shared a look, had she known what the look was for.

"Someone better start talking or I'm going to answer the door myself." When no one responded and Aiden was nowhere in sight, Danni got up to go answer the door. Even before she answered, she knew who it was.

"Honey, I'm home," Jaleen said as soon as she opened the door. She didn't even have time to react when he pulled her into his arms and kissed her on her cheek.

"Ew, gross. Let me go." She lightly pushed on his chest.

"You know you like it," he whispered before letting her go.

"Has anyone ever told you that you're a pervert?"

"Has anyone ever told you that playing hard to get doesn't work if a man loves to chase?"

"Who says I'm playing hard to get? You couldn't get me even if you tried." Normally their banter went back and forth like this for hours, but today, his silence caught her off guard. She turned toward him and placed her hands on her hips.

"What's wrong, Walker? Cat got your tongue?" She would have said more but the mischievous look in his eyes told her to stop while she was ahead.

"I can think of a lot of things I want to do with my tongue and each and every one of those things would bring you the utmost satisfaction."

She couldn't help the hitch in her breath at his innuendo. Apparently she wasn't thinking as quickly on her feet as she normally did. He glanced behind her before curling his hand around her waist and pulling her into a corner of the hallway. He leaned his forehead to hers in a way he never had before. The endearing gesture only made her breathing more staggered.

"I'm exhausted, but I needed to see you today," he said in a low voice. "I wouldn't have come if you weren't here."

Of all the years she'd known Jaleen, she couldn't recall a single time when she'd heard the vulnerability in his voice. It was then that she noticed the look of fatigue on his face and the small bags under his eyes. Without second-guessing herself, she raised a hand to smooth over his cheek. He leaned into her hand and briefly closed his eyes.

"I needed this," he said with his eyes still closed.

She wanted to say something back to him, but she didn't

know what to say. So instead she placed a soft kiss on his opposite cheek.

"Whatever is bothering you, it will be okay," she whispered when she finally found the words.

He opened his eyes and instead of the guarded—yet playful—playboy she usually saw, she recognized the man behind the sarcastic comments and charming demeanor. She saw the troubled man who had more questions right now than he had answers for. Uncertainty was written across his facial features, combating with the small part of himself that was hoping for a solution to his problems to magically appear. She understood the feeling all too well. She saw it in herself every time she looked in the mirror.

"Are you two just going to stand in the hallway all night? Or are you going to come and play cards?"

Both Danni and Jaleen turned toward the direction of Summer's voice. No one could see them, but she assumed they'd heard their footsteps when they'd stopped right outside the dining room.

"We're coming," Danni yelled as she dropped her hand from Jaleen's face. He squinted in disappointment. She was two seconds away from telling him they would continue whatever the heck just happened later, before she caught herself.

"We're playing Spades," Danni said to Jaleen. "But this is our last round. I guess you and Aiden can play whoever the winner is."

"Sounds good," he said, studying her eyes. She wasn't sure what he was looking for, but was relieved when he began walking toward the dining room.

At the end of the third round, Danni and Summer had taken the win.

"On that note," Nicole said as she stood from the table, "I think I'm going to call it a night."

"Me, too," Aaliyah said, standing, as well. "I'll see you ladies in the morning."

After Nicole and Aaliyah left, Jaleen and Aiden took their spots.

"Jay, since you're the newbie tonight, I have to warn you that Summer and I are a force to be reckoned with in Spades." Jaleen gave Danni a funny look.

"What's that look for?" she asked.

"You've never called me Jay. No other woman has ever called me that."

She nervously bit her bottom lip. "Is that a bad thing? If you don't like it, I'll call you something else."

"No, it's fine," Jaleen said with a smile. "You can call me whatever you want."

"Great, thanks."

Great? Thanks? Okay, Danni. Snap out of it!

When it came to cards, better yet, when it came to anything, she was competitive, not polite. However, thirty minutes into the game, it was evident that Jaleen was throwing her off her game. Not only were they barely talking smack to one another, but everyone was barely talking at all.

"Can you pass the pitcher of sangria?" Jaleen asked.

"Sure," Danni said as she passed the pitcher. "Can you pass the pretzels?"

"Of course." Jaleen passed her the bowl and a small plate to put the pretzels on.

"That's it," Summer said as she placed her cards face-down on the table. "Who are you guys and what have you done with the real Danni and Jaleen?"

"What do you mean?" Danni asked, although she knew exactly what Summer meant.

"Usually you both would have insulted each other at least ten times by now. Aiden and I are afraid to even speak because the sexual tension in the room is so high and, trust me, it's not us."

"Well, it's kind of us, too," Aiden said, winking at Summer. "But I agree with my wife. You two are sucking the fun out of the game. So how about we take a break? Summer and I will take a walk along the beach while you two work out whatever is going on."

"You think you're slick," Jaleen said when Aiden helped Summer out of her chair. "My guess is your plan was to get Summer to take a late-night walk with you on the beach all along."

"You have your methods and I have mine." A look passed between the two men that didn't go unnoticed by Danni.

Suddenly they were all alone with only the faint sound of the ocean in the distance seeping through the cracked window.

"What do you say we play two-person Spades until they get back?" Danni suggested. Anything was better than sitting in silence for the rest of the night.

"I'm game for that idea," Jaleen said, reaching for the cards. "What if we up the ante with a friendly bet to start off our friendship journey?"

What is he up to now? "What kind of bet?"

He kept his eyes trained on her as he shuffled the cards. "As much as you hate to admit it, the chemistry between us is undeniable. So I propose that we do something about it."

She adjusted herself in her chair, a little anxious about the turn in conversation. She'd spent the past few years trying to ignore their obvious attraction, so she couldn't deny his words. "I'm listening."

He placed the deck facedown on the table and popped a couple pretzels into his mouth. The act shouldn't have been sexy, but even watching him chew was getting to her. "I want to take you out on a date."

"That's the bet?" she said with a laugh. "We've been on a date before."

"I'm not talking about a date where all our friends are present. I'm talking about a date with just the two of us. Tell me something…" he said, standing to take the chair Aiden had just vacated so that they were sitting right next to one another. "When was the last time you were on a date with a man and truly enjoyed yourself?"

Almost never, she thought. "I've been on a few decent dates lately," she said instead. The disbelief in his eyes was immediate. Soon, the disbelief turned to understanding. It took all her effort not to jump in her seat when he touched her hand.

"Let me try a different approach. How long have we known each other?"

"Um, about three years, I think." *Actually, about three years, two months and twenty-seven days…not that I'm counting.*

"And in that time, have you ever thought of me in a nonfriendship way?"

Her mind raced to the first conversation they'd ever had. She'd been living in Chicago at the time, managing the Bare Sophistication boutique. She'd been the first to arrive at a local nightclub to meet up with Winter and Autumn for a girls' night out, when Jaleen had approached her at the bar.

She'd known who he was immediately since she'd seen him around Chicago with his best friend Taheim. At the time she was surprised when, instead of sitting next to her on a bar stool, he went behind the bar to make her a drink. Now that she knew Taheim's brother Ajay owned the club, it didn't seem too extreme, but at the time, she hadn't known what to make of his behavior. So she'd done what she did best. Told him off and ignored their attraction. Had she known he'd become a constant person in her life over the years, she may have reacted differently.

"What happens if I admit that I've thought of you in nonfriendship ways before?"

His eyes flickered with something she couldn't interpret. "Then I'd tell you that I propose that you allow me to take you on five dates."

Five dates? Seems simple enough. "And what would happen on these five dates?"

He observed her once more before responding. "For years we've been tiptoeing around each other, so these five dates would give us a chance to act on our attraction."

"And there's the catch," she said, shaking her head. "I assume you expect each date to end in sex."

"No, not necessarily, although I'm not counting it out." He winked at her. "These five dates would be more like fantasy dates. A chance for us to have a good time without worrying about the fact that we share a lot of mutual friends and the fact that we don't want to ruin our friendship. It would give us a chance to experience what it would be like if you hadn't turned me down the first night we met."

She studied his eyes, noting the sincerity in them. How many times had she wondered what it would be like to be the object of Jaleen's attention? How often had she wondered what it would be like to be intimate with him? True, this wasn't exactly what she'd expected if, in the rare case, they did decide to date. But she couldn't deny that the idea intrigued her.

"So if you win, we go on five fantasy dates. And if I win...?"

He scrunched his forehead in thought before snapping

his fingers. "I got it. If you win, you pick five days in which I'll cater to your every need."

"Hmm, that sounds really similar to what you'd get if you won."

His eyes darkened. "I was thinking more like I'd do chores around your house, pick up your clothes from the cleaner's or do your grocery shopping. But whatever you want, I'll give."

Oh, come on! He knew how he meant it and so did she. She glanced at the cracked-open window, contemplating what she should do. If she agreed to the bet, it seemed that, no matter what, they would be spending five days together. If she declined the bet, she'd always wonder if she missed the chance to give in to her attraction to Jaleen because she had no doubt that if they were back in Chicago, she would have never even contemplated agreeing to this.

Be careful. You have a lot at stake by getting close to a man like him.

She wasn't worried about getting attached to Jaleen. She could handle guarding her heart. What did worry her was the fact that even though they shared mutual friends, neither Jaleen nor those friends knew the truth about her past. True, her parents and brothers were amazing people and her family had accepted the mistakes she'd made. At least, the mistakes they knew about. However, her friends from Chicago and Miami didn't know what poor decisions she'd made over the past few years that had placed her in her current predicament. In fact, she was pretty sure that if Jaleen did know her secrets, he wouldn't be making this particular bet right now.

If she listened to that inner warning, she'd make the right decision and say no to what he was offering. Too bad that inner voice wasn't loud enough to shout over the other part of her that was too enthralled with what Jaleen was offering to say no.

She smiled despite how nervous she felt. "Okay, Walker, you have a deal." Her smile dropped the minute she shook his hand. His eyes were filled with promise, excitement and a fair warning that she be prepared for whatever he had in store.

Why do I feel like I just signed a deal with the devil?

Chapter 4

"I can't believe I lost," Danni said for the third time that morning. She could still see the look of accomplishment on Jaleen's face last week when he'd won the game. Even worse, he'd had the nerve to do a happy dance around the dining room table, chanting that he'd won.

She would have thought his excitement was flattering had she not been a nervous wreck ever since that night. When he'd called to ask if she was free the entire Sunday, her initial thought had been to decline an all-day date. But the Jaleen she knew would never plan to spend all day with a woman, so she'd accepted out of curiosity. Four days after accepting, she was still nervous.

She glanced at her outfit in her bathroom mirror. Jaleen hadn't given her a dress code, so she'd chosen to wear her favorite lavender romper and beige wedges. Instead of tying her hair up, she let her soft curls flow around her shoulders. Just as she lifted her eyeliner to apply some light makeup, a loud noise echoed through the wall.

"Oh, crap," she said as she dropped her eyeliner in the sink. Orchestra music rebounded off her walls from the condo next door. When Summer had moved in with Aiden, Danni had accepted Summer's offer to rent her condo.

Danni had lived there with Summer for a short while when she'd initially moved to Miami, so she was familiar with most of the neighbors. Unfortunately the one she shared a wall with was the hardest to get along with.

"Mr. Higgins," she said, banging on the wall. "Can you please turn down the music?" She'd thought they had an understanding after their last chat a couple weeks ago. Apparently there was no getting through to Mr. Higgins.

She reached into her drawer for the earplugs she'd purchased after one too many restless nights.

She'd just finished her makeup and taken out her earplugs when there was a knock at the door. "Hi, Jaleen," she yelled. "Come on in."

"Why is your neighbor's music so loud?" he yelled back. "I was just about to call you because I'd been knocking for a while."

"Sorry about that. I had in earplugs. My neighbor Mr. Higgins loves to play his music loudly three days a week. I thought I'd get used to it, but it still catches me off guard."

"Oh, yeah," Jaleen said with a laugh. "I think I remember Summer complaining about that guy one time." He stopped laughing and looked her up and down.

"You look beautiful," he yelled just as the music stopped. They both laughed.

"Thank you," she said with a smile. "You look nice, as well." He was wearing dark jeans and a blue shirt. "I've always liked you in blue."

A smile spread across his face. "Then I'll have to remember that for the future." She was sure he meant future dates, but just mentioning the word made her feel warm and tingly in places she had no business feeling warm and tingly. The music started back up, breaking the moment.

"Let's get out of here," she said, grabbing her purse and sweater.

Once they were in the car, her nervousness eased. "You know, the girls laughed when I told them about the bet."

"Considering our track record, I'm sure they did," Jaleen said with a laugh. "But I'm really looking forward to today."

"Me, too. Are you going to tell me where we're going?"

Jaleen glanced from the road to her. "Did you bring an appetite, like I asked?"

At the time she hadn't known if he'd meant an appetite for him or an appetite for food. Luckily, she'd brought an appetite for both.

Jaleen smirked. "Your mind is so dirty, Danni."

She waved her arms in innocence. "What? I didn't say anything."

"Yeah, well, I can read what you're thinking."

She observed him as he drove. "Probably because you're thinking the same thing I am."

The rest of the twenty-minute drive was in silence. As they parked in a lot in Little Havana, Danni was still clueless about the day date.

"Since you grew up in Miami, I'm assuming you already know where we are."

Danni turned to face Jaleen. "You remember that I grew up in Miami?"

He opened his door and went around the car to open hers. "I remember everything you tell me," he said as he helped her out the car. "Just like I remember that you're a vegetarian."

Danni squinted. "Little Havana is known for its Cuban cuisine and doesn't exactly have many vegetarian options."

"See, that's where you're wrong," he said as she looped her arm in his. "I happen to have a friend who specializes in vegetarian Cuban cuisine."

"You're kidding," Danni said with a smile. "Why haven't I heard of a vegetarian chef here before?"

"Probably because she doesn't advertise it. Her vegetarian dishes are by special request only."

"How do you know her?"

"I flipped a house a few years back that she brought. She also gives cooking lessons out of the guest house on the property, so we kept in touch." Jaleen led her to a small restaurant that already had people lining up on the sidewalk despite the fact it wasn't even the afternoon yet. Instead of getting in line, they bypassed the people and entered the restaurant.

"Jaleen, honey, so nice to see you again." Danni unlinked Jaleen's arm so he could hug the eccentric woman who was wearing about ten different vibrant colors. Danni knew exactly who she was and had watched her cooking shows when she was on the Food Network channel. Artemela Rojas wasn't only known for her unique Cuban cuisine, but also her flamboyant personality and fun-loving spirit. There weren't too many people who rendered Danni speechless upon meeting them, but Artemela was one of those people.

"Hello, Danni. I've heard so much about you." She pulled Danni in for a hug.

"Nice…to…uh, meet you," Danni finally got out. "I'm…so…uh, so honored."

A quick glance at Jaleen proved he was amused by the situation. "Artemela, Danni isn't aware of everything we're doing today and I'd like to keep it that way."

"Oh, I love surprises," Artemela said, clasping her hands together. "We have to open the restaurant, but I have the perfect spot for you."

Danni and Jaleen followed her to the rooftop where there sat a table in the corner with the perfect view of Little Havana. Two mimosas were waiting for them and a plate of spinach empanadas.

"Enjoy this appetizer while I get to work in the kitchen. Carlos will come check on you soon and I'll be back up later." After they both thanked Artemela, Danni was finally able to soak in what had just happened.

"Oh, my goodness, I can't believe I just hugged Artemela Rojas. She's legendary here in Miami. I knew she had some signature vegetarian dishes because I've followed her recipes for years, but this is beyond unbelievable."

"She's one of your favorite chefs, right? You used to watch her shows on television."

How did he know that? "Yes, she's one of my favorite chefs." She shook her head in disbelief. "I really have no idea how you knew that... I don't think I've ever talked about her before."

Jaleen took a sip of his mimosa, never breaking eye contact. "Do you remember the time we were at Ajay and Autumn's house discussing their wedding plans right after they got engaged?"

"Of course," she said, taking a sip of her mimosa, as well. "Winter and Taheim were trying to convince them to have a big wedding. But they were both insistent on not having an elaborate wedding."

"Exactly. We spent all night trying to dwindle down their wedding list to under one hundred people."

"Which was almost impossible," Danni said. "We decided to shelve that conversation for later."

Jaleen nodded his head in agreement. "So we all went to Ajay and Autumn's living room to watch a basketball game that was on and you offered to wash dishes in the kitchen. I eventually went to the kitchen to help and you were watching reruns of Artemela's show and unloading a bag full of groceries."

"Oh, right," she said, taken aback that he remembered. "When I was picking up food for the wedding planning session, I had picked up ingredients for a new dish that Artemela was making on the rerun that aired that night. You asked me if I loved cooking shows and I told you—"

"Only if it's an Artemela Rojas cooking show," Jaleen finished. "I wanted to tell you then that I knew her, but I was too wrapped up in observing your behavior."

She looked into his eyes, trying to process everything he was saying. "And what did you see that night? After observing me?"

He slightly squinted. "I'm not sure you want to know."

"Oh, come on," she said, playfully hitting his arm. "Now I'm curious. You have to tell me."

He didn't say anything for a few moments and she feared that he'd never tell her what he'd observed that day.

"I noticed a couple things," he finally said. "But the most important was the way your eyes lit up after you finished creating the dish. It couldn't have taken you any longer than thirty minutes, yet the way your eyes gleamed with excitement, you would have thought the dish had taken hours to complete."

She swallowed the sudden lump in her throat, determined to maintain eye contact. "You watched me for the entire thirty minutes?"

He gave her a sheepish grin as he shifted in his seat. "If I say I watched you for longer than that, would it creep you out?"

It doesn't, but maybe it should. "It actually creeps me out more that I didn't notice you watching me. I guess I'm more passionate about those cooking shows than I realized."

"I have a feeling that you're passionate about a lot more

than cooking shows," Jaleen said in a low voice. "But don't worry. I plan on finding out just how deep that passion goes."

The five-course vegetarian meal that Artemela had prepared had been everything Jaleen had hoped it would be. With each course, Danni's eyes had lit up more and more. After the meal, he'd taken her to his favorite gelato place in Miami. He couldn't remember the last time he'd had so much fun on a date. He glanced over at the woman who was responsible for one of the most carefree and enjoyable dates he'd ever had.

"So what's next?" she asked excitedly. "I'm not sure I can eat much more food, but I'd like to try." The sun was setting, which meant it was the perfect time to execute the last part of their first date. He hadn't had a chance to talk to Danni about the bucket list she'd mentioned to him months ago, but he didn't need to bring it up during this date. He knew at least one item on the list, but he was hoping his next suggestion would be something off her list. He'd be able to tell based on her facial expressions.

"I have a question for you before we do the last thing. Have you ever snuck onto a tour bus or into a concert?"

She looked at him inquisitively. "That's a strange question. I guess, no, I've never done either one."

"Have you ever thought about doing anything like that? Breaking the rules by sneaking into someplace you didn't belong?" He studied the way her eyebrows rose before she smiled.

"Actually, I have always wanted to sneak into a movie theater. You know, pay for one movie and then when it's over, sneak into another."

Perfect. "Well, luckily for you, that's exactly what I had planned." He grabbed her hand and led her to a local movie theater that only played two movies a night. Sneaking into a movie theater this small would definitely give them a rush and, if his plan worked, the item he'd placed earlier would still be waiting in the larger theater.

"Did you really have to pick the smallest theater in Miami?" Danni said as they approached the side door. "What if we get caught?"

"All they can do is kick us out," Jaleen said as they hid between the theater and another building. "Around this time, an employee should come out here to dump the trash. If it's the same guy who has worked the last couple nights, he'll prop open the door, so that's our window to rush in."

"Are you insane?" Danni whispered, looking over her shoulder at the people in the distance. "You promised me a fantasy date, not an illegal date."

"Being fed by your favorite chef was a fantasy. Besides, sneaking into an eight-dollar movie isn't that big of a deal. We'll be fine."

On cue, the door was propped open and the employee went to take out the garbage. "Showtime," Jaleen said as they sneaked through the door and hid in a darkened corner. Once the employee closed the door and went back to work, Jaleen held Danni close as they made their way to the movie theater. When they were in the clear, they blended in with the crowd in the lobby.

"See, that wasn't so bad, right?" he asked.

"I guess not, but that was still nerve-racking."

"Excuse me, sir," a voice said from behind them. Jaleen watched Danni's eyes widen in fear.

"May I help you?" Jaleen asked as he turned around. He held Danni's hand, trying to ease her nerves.

"Can you take our picture?" the man asked as he and his companion pointed to a life-size advertisement for an upcoming movie.

Danni loosened her grip on his arm.

"Sure." After snapping a few photos, he led Danni to the top corner of the movie theater. Luckily, no one had taken the seats nearest a wall fixture even though the movie was going to start soon. He lifted his hand to grab the bag he'd placed there.

"What are you doing?" she whispered.

"Getting this," he said as he sat next to her and untied the bag of cheese-and-caramel popcorn. "I figured you may miss Garrett's popcorn from Chicago, so I brought some down with me and hid a bag in this theater for us."

She shook her head in disbelief. "I can't express how much you've surprised me today," Danni said, accepting the bag he handed her. "And, yes, I've missed Garrett's since I've been here."

She was still looking into his eyes as the movie started. He couldn't read every emotion, but he read the most prominent one…gratitude.

I wish I could see this look in her eyes every day.

He tried to ignore the voice in the back of his mind but as she curled into his arm and dug into her popcorn, it was the only thought that remained.

Chapter 5

"JW, I'll be in Chicago in a couple weeks. Can it wait until then?"

"No, this meeting can't wait. First, you spend four months in Europe—"

"Which you agreed upon," Jaleen interrupted. Getting a call from his father early in the morning was never a good sign.

"I agreed to a month so that you could clear your mind. Not almost half of a year so you could frolic with European women."

Jaleen ran a frustrated hand down his face as he stared out into the ocean. His first instinct had been to ignore his father's call. He wished he'd followed his first mind.

When he'd initially decided to rent the luxury Miami penthouse on the eleventh floor, he was hoping it would bring more privacy than his massive Chicago penthouse because his family couldn't bother him in Miami like they did in Chicago. Too bad they'd followed him here. Ever since he'd arrived in Miami, he'd received daily at least two phone calls from either his father, uncle or brothers.

"I did not spend my time in Europe frolicking with

women. But, okay, if it's so important that we meet this week, I'll fly out first thing in the morning."

"Good decision," his father said right before he heard the dial tone.

"Nice chatting with you, too, JW," Jaleen said to himself as he slipped his phone in the pocket of his jogging pants. The only good thing about waking up early on a much-needed day off was getting a chance to see the sun rise. *It would be nice if Danni were seeing this with me.* He wasn't surprised at the thought. The date they'd had a few days ago had gone better than he'd expected. So good that he couldn't wait to see her again.

He was hoping he could take Danni on their second date this weekend, however, with the unexpected meeting his father had called, he doubted there would be time. *Unless we have a slight change of plans and she comes with me.* He wondered if a sudden trip to Chicago would be something she'd be interested in. Even if she was interested, he wasn't sure she could get away from Bare Sophistication for the weekend.

Jaleen took his phone out of his pocket and dialed Danni's number. He smiled the minute her honeyed voice reached his ears.

"Do you always make morning calls?"

He smiled. "Good morning to you, too, Danni. I was actually calling because I have to go to Chicago this weekend."

"Oh, okay." *Do I hear a hint of disappointment?* "No worries, we can reschedule our date… Or just forget about the whole rest of your bet and I can put you to work on my chores." *And she's back.*

"No, I'm not calling to reschedule. I'm calling to ask if you would accompany me to Chicago this weekend." After a lengthy silence, he repeated himself.

"I know you still have your penthouse, but I'm currently renting my condo. Where would we stay?"

"I have two extra bedrooms at my place, so you could stay with me."

"Are you sure staying with you at your place is a good idea?"

"Or, I guess a hotel is always an option. But, I think sharing the same space for a couple days is a great idea. If it makes you feel more comfortable, you can have the bedroom on the first floor instead of the bedroom down the hall from me." He glanced over to his left. "Besides, we're already practically neighbors, so this should be easy."

"What are you talking about?"

He angled his head over his balcony. "Look up to your right and tell me what you see."

"Are you kidding me?" she yelled a few seconds later. "You moved into the building right next to me? Are you insane?"

"Nope, I'm not insane. Out of all the places I saw, this was the best condo in the best location. It just happened to be next to where you lived." He laughed as he observed her. Even though he couldn't make out her facial features, her body language proved she was annoyed. Since he wanted her to accompany him to Chicago, telling her that they lived in complexes adjacent to one another may not have been the smartest decision, but he couldn't take it back now.

"Come on, Danni," he pleaded. "Head back to Chicago with me for the weekend. I really enjoyed our first date and I'd love to keep our plans for our second."

"I'll have to think about it and call you back."

As they disconnected the call, Jaleen decided to take a shower. Showers always helped clear his mind and in this case, he had to think of a way to convince her to join him if her answer was leaning more toward no. After a couple hours, she finally called him back.

"Okay," she said with a sigh. "I'll go with you, but here's the deal. For months, Summer and I have been trying to see if we could land a meeting with an up-and-coming Spanish swimsuit designer, Christian Serrano. We'd love to carry Christian's designs in both Bare Sophistication stores and word is, Serrano has agreed to allow boutique stores to carry the latest Christian Serrano collection as opposed to larger retail chains. An hour ago, we finally received the good news. So I can go with you to Chicago… if you don't mind spending a couple days with me in Barcelona. Our options were meeting Christian in Barcelona, or waiting until the Miami Swim and Lingerie Show this summer. Summer and I really don't want to lose out and you are more familiar with Europe than I am."

Jaleen did a fist pump in the air. He really didn't have a couple days to spare, but he also didn't want to pass up the opportunity to spend some time in Barcelona with Danni.

"When is your meeting with Christian Serrano?."

"I was waiting to talk to you first."

"I technically can move my business meeting up to tomorrow if you want to head to Barcelona on Saturday."

"That would work! I'll call Christian's manager and see if a Sunday or Monday meeting would work."

They discussed the details to book flights to both Chicago and Barcelona before hanging up. At first, Jaleen had been dreading the upcoming meeting at Walker Partner Realty. Now, he couldn't wait to get the meeting over with so he could spend time with Danni.

"Hey, watch where you're going," Danni yelled as she jumped out of the way of folks on a Segway tour. Being back in Chicago felt great, but she had to admit she didn't miss the constant need to dodge people on the sidewalks or streets. Miami was a fast-paced city, but nothing like the hustle and bustle of downtown Chicago.

Her flight with Jaleen had just landed a couple of hours ago and already he'd had to leave for an important meeting with his family. He'd gotten several calls while they were commuting to his place. The minute they'd dropped their bags off in his penthouse, she'd felt Jaleen's tension rise even more when he received yet another call. She'd wished there was something she could do to ease his aggravation, but he'd shuffled out of the apartment quicker than she could formulate comforting words.

Rather than stay cooped up in Jaleen's penthouse, she decided to visit Winter and Autumn at Bare Sophistication since it was only a mile from Jaleen's home. She was almost to the boutique when her phone rang with a number she didn't recognize.

"Hello?"

There was a slight pause on the other line. "I need to speak to Danni." The voice was direct and left no room for questioning what type of call it was.

"This is she," Danni said hesitantly. "May I ask who's calling?" She heard ruffling on the other end.

"So it's true. You did block my number," another voice different than the first said in an irritated tone. *Oh, no, please don't let it be who I think it is.* "Glad I decided to call you from my friend's phone, although I must say, Danni, I'm surprised you had the guts to block me."

Danni stepped off the main sidewalk and walked toward the moderate opening between two buildings. She closed her eyes, hoping she'd just imagined the call.

"You've already said hello so I know you can hear me. And I know you're well aware that you are late delivering my money."

"I'm not late with your money," Danni said, finally getting over the shock of the call. "Every month you call earlier than the month before. Our agreement was that I would pay you every fourth week, not third."

"Oh, really?" the caller said in disbelief. "What makes you think you have any grounds to negotiate with me? I have nothing to lose. But you? You have everything to lose."

Danni leaned her head against the brick building as she tried to calm her rapidly beating heart. "I'm not paying you early," she said, standing her ground. "You'll get your money next week."

"I better get my money with interest," the caller said louder than before. "And I don't mean a shitty interest, either. It better be something worth all the hell you've put me through by blocking my number. And in case you pull any funny business, I hope you realize that I have connections and I know where you are."

Danni held the phone even closer to her ear. "Are you threatening me?" She was furious and, despite the mess she'd gotten herself into, she refused to be walked over.

"It's more than a threat. It's a promise. You think hiding out in Miami working at that crappy boutique will keep me from getting to you? Well, you're wrong. You have no idea what I'm capable of, but I have a few people who could give you some insight if you want."

How had it come to this? Danni wasn't sure she'd ever felt more helpless about a situation in her life. "Look, I'll contact you next week to make arrangements for your money. Until then, you can't keep calling me like this. I have a life and we made an agreement."

The malicious laugh on the other end of the line sent chills running down her spine. "Just have my damn money ready next week."

Danni flinched when the caller yelled a few choice words before hanging up. "Oh, no," she whispered when she felt another panic attack coming on. She'd been having panic attacks for over a year and no matter what she tried to do to de-escalate the problem in her mind, it never worked. She placed her hand over her heart as she pushed off from the wall. *It's okay, Danni. Just breathe.*

Fifteen minutes later she'd managed to calm her nerves as she walked into Bare Sophistication.

"Danni, we were hoping you'd stop by," Winter said, quickly bringing Danni in for a hug. "Miami looks good on you."

"You know I couldn't come to Chicago without stopping by," she said, returning the hug. "It looks like you could use a hand. Do you need me to step in?" The store was filled with women, compliments of the semiannual sale that was currently going on. Winter and Autumn even had a few of their signature spring lingerie sets on sale and they were flying off the racks.

"Hey, Danni," Autumn said, giving her a quick hug before she got back to helping customers.

"Help would be great." Winter handed her several lingerie pieces to fold or put back on the rack. "Two floor associates called in sick today and we have the other two on the registers."

"Just like old times," Danni said with a smile. She'd managed retail stores before but Bare Sophistication was the first store she'd ever managed in which the employees felt more like family than associates. The way that Winter and Autumn worked together to breathe life into such an amazing vision was something Danni couldn't have been more proud to be a part of. Although the Miami location was only a year old, it was obvious that the same camaraderie would be brought to that store, as well. Especially with Aaliyah and Nicole stepping in for the boudoir studio.

As she got to work, her mind drifted to Jaleen. *I should probably tell him I'm at the boutique.* While they had been on the plane, he'd mentioned that his meeting would only take a couple of hours. Judging by the chaos at Bare Sophistication, Danni felt like Winter and Autumn would need her help for a few more hours than that. She quickly sent him a text to let him know and he'd quickly texted back that he needed a little longer, as well.

After four hours of nonstop work, Danni, Winter and Autumn escaped to the back office.

"Okay, we only have about a twenty-minute break until we have to get back on the floor for the evening shift, so you better spill fast," Winter said as she plopped down next to Autumn on the sofa.

Danni squinted at Winter. "Exactly what am I spilling?" She took a seat in the chair adjacent to them.

"You know exactly what I'm talking about. How in the world did you agree to go on a date with Jaleen?"

"Summer told you?"

"Actually," Autumn said with a sly smile, "Jaleen called us an hour ago and asked if we'd occupy you a while longer before your date."

Danni's mouth dropped open. "Please tell me you're joking. He actually told you about the bet?"

Autumn glanced at Winter before turning up one eyebrow at Danni. "And what bet might that be?"

Crap, they didn't know. Summer and the girls in Miami already knew, so, technically, it wasn't a secret. However, making the bet in Miami where most of her friends were embarking on new journeys in their lives seemed a lot more innocent than news traveling around Chicago where everyone had known Jaleen and Danni for years as nothing more than friends.

"We've only gone on one date so far," Danni said as she fidgeted in her chair. "Long story short, Jaleen and I were playing cards and, if I lost, I had to go on five dates with him."

Winter laughed loudly. "That man has been trying to get you to agree to a date for years. I can't believe you finally gave in all because you lost a game of cards."

"It was best two out of three, so I actually lost two games." Instead of responding, they both regarded her with knowing looks.

"What?" she asked, tired of being out of the loop.

"You already know what," Autumn said. "And now you two are headed to Barcelona for a short trip? We may not know how things have been since Jaleen moved to Miami, but the chemistry between you two has always been obvious."

Danni leaned back, unable to deny she'd agreed to the bet for that same reason. She'd be the first to say that a woman could accomplish any and everything with or without a man. Even so, she'd gone without the comfort of being thoroughly kissed…thoroughly made love to…for entirely too long. Jaleen was on a mission and it didn't take a rocket scientist to see where these fantasy dates were headed. She was so lost in her own thoughts that she forgot Winter and Autumn were in the room until they spoke again.

"Yeah, she knows what's in store," Autumn replied, glancing at Winter.

"I don't know, Autumn." Winter crossed her arms over her chest. "Danni may have noticed their chemistry, but Jaleen has had years to prepare."

She swallowed. Hard. If what they were saying was true, these next four dates wouldn't go as smoothly as the first date. On their first date, Jaleen had probably been aiming to make her feel comfortable with the idea of them dating. Now that date one was out the way, there was no telling what he had planned next.

Chapter 6

Jaleen stared out the large floor-to-ceiling conference room window as he watched the moon slowly rise into place. He'd always known that he'd work in the family business. He loved the work that Walker Realty Partner did, however, over the past five years he no longer recognized the company as the one he'd once loved. The past two years had been far worse than the previous three.

Jaleen didn't think his family understood that he also had another business to run. He was a partner at R&W Advertising along with his friends Taheim Reed and Daman Barker. Both men had other businesses to attend to, as well. However, they'd taken over several of his larger clients when he'd needed to dedicate more time to Walker Realty Partner.

Jaleen had been very close to his grandfather and he'd always envisioned taking over the company one day. Realistically, he knew that being the youngest of three brothers meant that his dream may never be a reality, but his brothers were content with their roles in the company and his grandfather had groomed Jaleen to take over one day.

When he'd found out that his grandfather had lung cancer, he'd been devastated. It was no secret that his grandfather had enjoyed smoking cigars. Whereas most people had a wine room, his grandfather had a cigar room, full of cigars from all over the world. Any time Jaleen went someplace, he brought him at least two cigars…one to smoke and one for his collection.

His grandfather had always joked that if old age didn't knock him off his rocker, smoking would. They only had six months with him before he passed. Jaleen had spent every day at the hospital leading up to his grandfather's death. The last promise he'd made his grandfather was to make sure he always did what was best for Walker Realty Partner. His grandfather had dedicated his life to building the Walker brand and there was no way that Jaleen was going to see the company fail.

"Jaleen, what's the status of the South Beach project?"

Jaleen cleared his throat before responding to his father. "We're a little behind schedule, but I'm confident that my team can make the deadline."

"Good, because I'm sending an appraiser to South Beach in a few weeks."

Sending an appraiser in a few weeks is way too soon. "That's too soon. Although things are running smoothly, I think it would be best if you wait until I give the okay before sending an appraiser." Jaleen glanced at his brothers and uncle who were also present in the conference room, but neither man commented on his behalf. He really couldn't blame them. Trying to reason with JW was like trying to outrun the wind. Exhausting and impossible.

His father looked up from the documents he was reviewing. "If things are going as smoothly as you specified, then a few weeks is more than enough time."

Things weren't going as well as Jaleen had hoped, so having an appraiser looming over him, calculating his every decision, was not what he needed. However, trying to get Jael Walker to understand that he had everything under control, despite a couple of major setbacks, would be a hard promise to sell. Jael Walker didn't know the meaning of failure, nor did he know the meaning of setbacks. Growing up, Jaleen used to admire his father's stern business attitude and the fact that everyone seemed to respect him in the real-estate industry. Little had he known at the time that although some may respect the man better known as JW, they'd feared him more than anything.

"Just promise me you'll give me a heads-up when the appraiser will be sent." It would be a waste of breath to continue to argue about the same topic.

"I'm not sure I like that tone in your voice," Jael said. "Seems you've forgotten your place while you've been away."

Jaleen counted to ten in his head as he reminded himself why he put up with his father's disrespect. Even now, Jaleen still had flashbacks about the meeting his family had had with his grandfather's lawyer after he'd died. The meeting in which they'd learned JW was to run the company, not Jaleen as they'd all suspected.

JW may be the current president of Walker Partner Realty, but Jaleen had no doubt in his mind that he would be a better leader than his father. Unfortunately he had to play his cards right before he set his sights on overthrowing JW from the throne he'd placed himself on.

"JW, can we try to conclude this meeting in a civil manner?"

JW disregarded his question and continued discussing business.

Jaleen observed his father, wondering when their once good relationship had turned into a poor replica of itself. A quick glance at his brothers, Jeremiah and Joel, made him wonder if they felt the same way. Years of being bossed around by their father was evident in the stress lines on their faces. Being the youngest did award him a certain benefit of seeing what they each went through when dealing with the wrath of JW. He was able to prepare himself for what he knew was coming if things didn't change with JW.

"Jaleen, need I remind you that you turn thirty-five in less than six months?"

"I'm well aware of my birthday."

JW clasped his hands in front of him. "Then you're also well aware that this so-called lifestyle you're living will cease soon."

Jaleen was already shaking his head. "Not until my birthday."

The look on JW's face made Jaleen take pause. He'd seen the look on his father more times than he could count and he had a feeling he wasn't going to like what his father was about to say.

"Jaleen, I've had enough of your disrespect. I won't have you stand in the way of furthering our family's business."

"I'm not standing in the way of anything. I understand what's at stake, which is why I simply want to do my job without having one of your goons watching my every move. You know the type of work I'm capable of. I always deliver—and this South Beach project will be one of our best property flips yet."

The tension on Jael's face seemed to ease a little. "For your sake, you better hope you're right. There will be consequences if you're wrong."

"And there it is, gentlemen," Jaleen said, waving his hands around the room. "First threat of the night. Honestly, I'm surprised it didn't happen hours ago."

Jaleen knew he was playing with fire. JW never liked to be baited, but after over seven hours of being in the room with his brothers, uncle and JW, he was beginning to lose his patience.

"Don't be such a pompous ass," JW said with a spiteful smirk. "Maybe you should try acting your age for a change."

Jaleen flinched. "I'll start acting my age when you start running this business like Grandfather used to."

JW's smirk immediately dropped. Mentioning their grandfather had always been an emotional trigger for JW.

"Let's sunset this conversation and move on to the next order of business," Jaleen's uncle suggested.

"No need," Jaleen said as he rose from his seat. "I have other important business to tend to tonight, so I have to go. Jeremiah will fill me in on what I missed."

He left before anyone could say anything else, especially JW. He knew that coming to Chicago would be stressful but, as usual, Jaleen had underestimated the effect his father had on him. Maybe subconsciously he'd known that he'd feel emotionally and physically drained after meeting with his family, which was why he'd asked Danni to accompany him on the trip. He was excited to see her, but he had so much weighing on his heart that he wasn't sure he'd be good company.

Jaleen pulled out his phone and began calling a number he hadn't dialed in a couple of weeks. On the third ring, the caller answered. "Hello? Jaleen, is this you?"

"Yes, it's me. Hi, Mom. How are you?"

"So much better now that you called. Oh, wait," she said a little more panicked. "Is everything okay with you? Are your brothers okay?"

"Everyone is fine, Mom. I just called because…" His voice trailed off. "I honestly don't know why I called. I just needed to hear your voice, I guess. I'm glad you finally have phone service."

"Me, too. We'll be in Beijing for at least another couple weeks," his mom said. "Then we head deep into a Thailand rain forest, so I probably won't have service again."

When his mother—former history professor—had originally told him and his brothers that she was celebrating her retirement by backpacking around the world for two years with a group of historians, they'd thought she was joking. Now, a year into her two-year trek, she seemed more dedicated than ever.

"That's great, Mom. I'm glad you're living your life. Somebody in this family should be." He grew quiet then, wrapped up in his own thoughts.

"Oh, sweetie, I think I know why you called. I'm guessing your father is being even more unreasonable than usual since your birthday is approaching in a few months."

Jaleen closed his eyes and sighed as he thought about the way his mother always knew exactly what was wrong without him even saying much. Jocelyne Walker may not win a Pulitzer for best mom of the year, but she'd put up with Jael Walker for over thirty years. She deserved an award for having to endure that man for as long as she did. It wasn't until he became an adult that Jaleen realized that his mother had only been distant with her sons because she knew nurturing them would only make JW push them harder.

"You guessed it," he said.

"And your brothers and uncle understand, but aren't really supporting you when you try to stand up to your father."

"Exactly." Jaleen hopped into his car, racing through the parking garage faster than he should. It always seemed that way when he was leaving the office. The Walker Realty Partner parking garage wasn't someplace you left leisurely. With Jael Walker as an owner, you left as fast as you could.

"Jaleen, I know you don't want to hear this, but you have to stand up to your father at some point. You can't let him rule your life like this."

"I know that, but you of all people understand how difficult that is."

"But, Jaleen, out of all three of my sons, you are the one who can reach your father. You are the one who always had the qualities and makings to be better at the real-estate business than he ever was, and for that reason alone, your father has always been slightly afraid of what you can accomplish."

What his mother was saying wasn't news to him. He'd heard it before from Jeremiah. Her words should have motivated him to finally stand up to his father. Instead they only made him more frustrated.

"JW's been like this all his life. No matter what I say or do, he will still expect me to fall in line after my thirty-fifth birthday."

"Your father wasn't always like this," Jocelyne said. "There was a time in his life when he never would have traded his soul for the business."

"Then what happened?" Jaleen asked as he parked his car outside of Bare Sophistication. "I remember the stories you used to tell us about how great a man he was, but I've never seen that man."

"Rarely anybody does," she said with a sigh. "But I think that man may still be buried deep inside there. In the meantime, why don't you try and do something that can take your mind off of your father and the business. Maybe even think to take a vacation."

Jaleen stepped out of his car, taken aback by the chilly night air. He hadn't been in Miami long enough to forget about the extremely cold spring days in Chicago, but he'd forgotten that even in the spring, it felt like there was always a chance of snow.

"Funny you should say that because I'm actually leaving for Barcelona tomorrow."

"Oh, really? For business?"

"More for pleasure than business."

"With a special someone perhaps?"

Jaleen didn't answer right away. "Perhaps."

"Well, I won't coax it out of you right now, but next time we talk, I expect you to tell me more."

After ending the call, he made his way into Bare Sophistication. He had a feeling Danni was still there helping Winter and Autumn with the semiannual sale.

He went to open the door, surprised that it was locked. "I guess it is really late," he said as he glanced at his watch. This was definitely not the night he had planned. He was just stepping away when he saw Danni come to the front of the store to get boxes. *Damn.* Even after a long day's work, she still looked beautiful. Her sleeveless white blouse was tucked into a fitted peach skirt and her hair was pinned in a clip. He knocked on the window until he got her attention.

"Jaleen, what are you doing here?" she asked as she unlocked the door, then locked it again after he entered the boutique. "I thought we were meeting at your place?"

"We were, but my meeting finally got out and I figured you'd be here since the sale was still going on."

"The sale ended a couple hours ago and I told Winter and Autumn I'd close up shop. A couple of employees are still here counting inventory in the back."

He glanced down at a few boxes on the ground. "Do you need help with these?"

"Actually, help would be great. I was restocking the displays, but these boxes have to go back in storage. There are about five boxes in the back of the store off to the side, as well."

"Just point me in the right direction," he said, lifting two boxes at a time. Usually after a business meeting with his family, working out would help him blow off his frustration, so he welcomed the easy labor. It took him less than ten minutes to clear the boxes off the floor. He then assisted Danni with straightening the racks of lingerie and dusting off the shelves before the other two employees came to help. Thirty minutes after his arrival, the store looked in tip-top shape.

"We'll head out through the back door," Danni said as she let the two associates out and turned off the lights. "Let me just turn on the alarm."

"Okay." Jaleen went to grab his discarded blazer and Danni's coat when he tripped over a box. "Are these boxes supposed to be behind the register or in storage?"

Danni walked around the counter and opened the boxes. "No, these are pieces from the latest collection, so they definitely need to be in storage."

Danni picked up his blazer and her coat as he grabbed a box and brought it to the storage.

"Do you want me to organize these boxes?" he yelled, noticing how unorganized it had gotten after the associates had done inventory.

"I can do that," Danni said, entering the storage room. "Can you grab the last of the boxes?"

"Sure." He made a couple more trips. "This is the last one." He went to drop it on top of the others, not noticing that Danni had placed one of the boxes on the floor. Hitting the door that had been propped open was the only thing to catch his fall.

"Sorry," Danni said, turning her head. "I thought you'd

see the box on the floor." All the color from her face drained.

"What's wrong?"

She pointed to the door. "Please tell me you unlatched the security lock before you let the door close."

Jaleen looked at the closed door. "I didn't unlatch anything. I hadn't planned to fall back on the door."

"Oh, crap," she said, running to the door. She pulled the handle and the door didn't budge. "Did you happen to grab my purse?"

"No, I didn't even see your purse."

"Shoot, I must have pushed it under the register when I went to look through those boxes." Danni tried to open the door with more force.

"Let me try." Jaleen grabbed the handle with even more force. "Why does this lock on the inside?"

"It's a security feature that's on a lot of storage doors. If you enable the security latch—sort of like a child's safety lock in a car—it will lock from the inside, trapping the intruder. Or in this case, us."

"There's no way we're trapped in here." Jaleen tried the handle again. "When does the store open tomorrow?"

"They may open at eight a.m. because of the sale, but I'm not sure. I didn't ask."

"Wouldn't they check on the store if they don't hear from you tonight?"

"Maybe, but it's hard to say since I never checked in with them when I closed the store before moving to Miami with Summer."

Jaleen squeezed the bridge of his nose as he felt a headache brewing. Being trapped in a storage room with Danni wasn't the worse thing to happen today, but the situation wasn't ideal. Usually he'd focus more on everything he could accomplish while being trapped with a beautiful woman, but he wasn't his normal self. He had entirely too much on his mind.

His current situation didn't have anything to do with JW, but it felt like, somehow, the universe was warning him not to play with fire because when it came to arguing with JW, one was sure to get burned. His mom felt like it was his time to stand up to his father. His brothers felt it was best for him to just leave well enough alone and fall into line. Whereas, he didn't know what the hell he was supposed to do.

"We have to get out of here. Our flight leaves tomorrow afternoon for Barcelona and even though they will probably find us in time, we can't stay here all night." The worry lines were evident on Danni's face. "Do you have your phone? We could call Winter or Autumn to let us out."

"Yeah." He grabbed his blazer and pulled out his phone. "And I still have more than fifty-percent battery."

"Great! Your phone should work in here, though the reception is horrible." Jaleen froze as he looked at his service bars.

"Don't tell me." Danni crossed her arms over her chest. "You don't have service."

He leaned against a couple of boxes. "Okay, then I won't tell you."

Chapter 7

After fifty-five minutes, it was evident that the night was not going to go by fast. Jaleen was leaning against the wall with his eyes closed. He'd been in that position for the past thirty minutes. Danni didn't want to admit it to herself, but she was a little surprised that he hadn't made a move on her yet. She figured being trapped with a playboy like Jaleen would give him the green light to try whatever moves he had, which she knew was a lot because she'd seen him in action. Not only had he not tried anything, they hadn't spoken since they learned his phone didn't have service.

"We used to joke that it would be funny if someone got trapped in here," Danni said, breaking the silence. "But that's never been an actual concern."

"Yeah, well, leave it to me to be the cause of something happening that was once only a joke between employees." His eyes remained closed as he spoke. Although the lighting in the storage room was dim, she noticed him clench and unclench his jaw. *Something's bothering him.* She'd felt it the minute he'd walked into the boutique, although he'd tried to disguise it by helping her fulfill the duties needed to close the shop.

She walked toward his direction and leaned next to him

on the wall. Even now, she could feel the tension emanating throughout his body. He still looked sexy as usual, but his facial features seemed tense, like he had the weight of the world on his shoulders.

"Is there a reason you're staring at me?"

She gasped when he spoke. "How did you know? You haven't opened your eyes in a while."

He opened his eyes then and turned to her. "Whenever we are in the same room, I am acutely aware of everything about you. Which side of the room you're on. If you're observing me or observing our friends. If you're uncomfortable, I can tell. If you're tense, I can tell."

She smiled. "Kind of like I can tell that you're tense right now." She studied his eyes. "What's wrong? Did your meeting not go as planned?"

The underlying irritation was evident. "No, it went exactly how I thought it would go."

"Do you want to talk about it?"

He looked away and blew out a frustrated breath. They didn't really have the type of friendship where they talked about their feelings. They'd had serious conversations before but, for the most part, those conversations had been kept light.

"As you may recall, my family's business, Walker Realty Partner, specializes in flipping real estate, among other things. I guess you can say that the past few years have been difficult for us and a lot is riding on my current project in South Beach." He sighed. "Unfortunately that's the least of my worries considering, after the completion of this project, I have even more obligations to fulfill for the company."

"I'm sure you can handle it," Danni said as she placed a supportive hand on his shoulder. "You're Jaleen Walker. There's nothing you can't do."

Her goal was to get him to laugh and she was rewarded by a hearty one. "I wish that were true." His face grew serious. "But this is a situation that I'm not sure I can get out of. My father is making it extremely difficult. I can't go into all the details, but he's the type of man that everyone listens to when he speaks. My brothers and uncle all listen to him, and even my mom does in some ways. If I disregard his wishes, the consequences of my decisions won't just affect him. They will affect the rest of the family and the business my grandfather built. Walker Partner Realty is our legacy. Besides their families, it's all my brothers live for right now. I'm not sure I could do that to them."

"But what about you?" She stepped closer to him. "What do you want?"

He closed his eyes again and leaned the back of his head against the wall. "I'd thought about it for years, and I think that the company as we know it is not going to last. We need to start over. We need to remember the foundations on which the company was started in the first place, rebuild our reputation and rebrand ourselves. If it were up to me, instead of trying to continue to prove to other competitors and businesses in the real-estate industry that we're the best, we'd admit failure and start over."

Danni ran the back of her hand over his cheek, enjoying the stubble that was starting to peek through. She'd always sensed that Jaleen had a lot of layers, but she was starting to realize there was so much more depth to him than she'd originally realized. *He always closes his eyes when he needs to get a handle on his frustration.* She hadn't seen him upset too many times but, looking back, she could recall several times when he'd come to a group outing after a business meeting and she'd caught him closing his eyes longer than necessary.

"In the past, I always thought that maybe you were tired

when you would join the group for drinks or dinner after a work meeting." She placed a quick kiss on his cheek. "But, looking back, it was your way of trying to control your frustration, right? We all know you as Jaleen the Jokester. Or Jaleen the Life of the Party. Even Jaleen the Man Who Never Takes Life Too Seriously. Now I see that all those times, it was your way of masking what was really going on."

He opened his eyes again, making her breath catch. "I wish I could tell you everything. And, if I'm being completely honest, I'm worried we'll lose our closeness if I do. There are some things about me that you don't know. Things no one really knows and wouldn't understand. I'm not sure you'll understand yet, either, and I don't want to risk that."

What could he possibly say that would make me turn my back on him? She wanted to ask, but she had secrets, too. Secrets she wasn't ready to share with anyone, even Jaleen.

"You're not ready to open up to me about certain things, either," he said as if reading her mind. "Am I right?"

She nodded her head. "Like you said, I'm not sure you'll understand yet. We only just began growing our friendship in a way that doesn't include bickering all the time or taking punches at each other."

"Is that all this is?" he asked. "A friendship?"

Her heart was screaming for her to tell him that she felt like it was more than a friendship. That she wasn't sure if the type of chemistry they had could be defined as a friendship or something a lot deeper than that. But her mind was warning her to tread lightly. Despite how close they were getting, she still had to be careful. There was so much about life that she still had to figure out. Important decisions she still had to make. However, in this moment, she didn't want to think too hard anymore. All she wanted to do was something she'd been wanting to do for weeks, years even.

Slowly her hand moved from his cheek to the back of his head. All she had to do was to lift up on her toes and tilt her head to his. The next steps seemed so simple, yet her nerves were getting the best of her. Luckily, Jaleen didn't seem to be going through the same inner struggle as she was. His arms wrapped around her waist and he pulled her to him.

Danni expected him to kiss her right away but instead he leaned his forehead to hers and took a deep breath before placing a soft kiss on her lips. Even though the kiss was tender, her arms prickled in goose bumps at the fact that she was finally kissing him after all this time.

When her other hand went around his neck, Jaleen slipped his tongue into her mouth and deepened the kiss. Kissing was something Danni had always enjoyed but never got enough of. Her problem in past relationships was the fact that she'd always enjoyed kissing much more than the person she was dating. Then again, none of them had ever had lips like Jaleen's. Soft yet firm. Sweet yet masculine. He knew when to apply pressure. He knew when to give more tongue. He knew when to pull back, enticing her to pull his head even closer.

When she moaned into his mouth, he pulled back. "When was the last time you were thoroughly kissed?"

She could barely stand let alone gather enough brain function to answer his question. "Are you seriously asking me this now?"

"I need to know," he said, brushing a few strands of hair out of her face that had escaped her clip. "You'll see why soon."

"Um." She scrunched her forehead. "I guess it's been a while. Years even."

He studied her face. "The night of the bachelor and bachelorette party, you asked me to kiss you. You said that I was on your list."

Her eyes widened. "I told you about my list?"

"Maybe," he said with a smirk. "You don't have to tell me more right now. Just elaborate on the part that includes me kissing you."

She tilted her head to the side. She wasn't surprised she'd mentioned her list. It seemed like she'd talked a lot that night. "Full disclosure?"

"Full disclosure."

She looked into his trusting eyes. "I've always enjoyed the art of kissing. The way that the perfect kiss can change the course of a relationship. To me, a kiss is more important than having sex with a person. Without a good kiss, it's harder for me to connect with my significant other." She briefly dropped her eyes to his lips. "In the past, I've been in relationships with men who didn't enjoy kissing like I enjoyed kissing. To them, it was more of a chore than a form of foreplay."

"That's unfortunate because all I've been thinking about since we met is how you taste."

She glanced away at the intensity of his stare. He lifted her chin so he could continue to gaze into her eyes. "So how exactly did I make this list?"

"I guess it was in the way your mouth moved when you talked."

"Really?" he asked with one upturned eyebrow. "The way I talked?"

"Yeah," she said sheepishly. "I guess you can say that part of the reason why I always enjoyed bickering with you is because I became enthralled with the way your mouth moved. The way it curved into a side smile. The secrets behind the way your lips moved. I felt like your lips were the type of lips that were made for kissing. The type of lips that a woman could get lost in. I guess you could say that the reason you made my list as the person I wanted to thoroughly kiss was because when I was concocting my list, there was no other name—no other pair of lips—that came to mind…but yours."

His deep brown eyes darkened to a shade she hadn't yet seen. "Let's see if I can live up to your expectations." She wanted to tell him that he already had. That their first kiss had already been extremely more satisfying than all the kisses she'd previously had. However, she didn't get the chance. He pulled her back into his embrace and braced one hand on her thigh. Their lips intertwined in a passionate kiss as his other hand tangled in her hair. On their own accord, her legs lifted off the floor and Jaleen was right there to catch her.

He gently placed her on the nearby boxes, never disconnecting their lips. *I was right*, she thought. *Lips like his were made for kissing.* The way he explored her mouth was intoxicating. She felt each nip of his teeth and lick of his tongue deep within her core.

Slowly she widened her thighs so that he could adjust himself between her legs. His hands left her hair and inched underneath her skirt, caressing her thighs. Jaleen kissed her as if they had all the time in the world, which, technically, she supposed they did since they were locked in the storage room. Unlike the kisses in her past that were uneventful, Jaleen's kisses seemed to tell a story. Within his kisses, she felt his frustration from the day he'd had. She felt his desire to confide in her more, as well as the restrictions he'd placed on himself to try to hold back so that he wouldn't scare her away. She couldn't uncover his secrets, but she felt the weight they placed on his heart.

Her moans echoed throughout the room, mingling with

the groans that escaped deep within his throat. This was it. This was the type of kiss she'd felt like she waited her entire life for. There wasn't any part of her mouth that felt untouched. His hands felt as divine as his lips, his thumbs rubbing soothing circles across her skin. She didn't stop his hands from traveling farther up her thighs, inching closer to the part that craved him with a fierceness she'd never felt before. Without warning, he broke the kiss and searched her eyes.

"Are you okay?" he asked. She nodded her head yes, unable to formulate words with his hand still near her core. She assumed he'd asked her another question because he looked as if he was still waiting for a response. Yet talking was the last thing she wanted to do. She wanted more. Needed more. She scooted closer to his fingers, hoping he got the hint that she wanted him to continue. When he raised a questioning eyebrow, she nodded her head again in agreement.

Since they weren't talking, she wasn't sure what she was agreeing to. All she knew was that she didn't want him to stop. She needed him to continue. The next look he gave her was a warning that she had about three seconds to stop him before he did whatever caused him to give her a sly grin. She returned his grin with one of her own. One that she hoped said *I'm game for whatever you've got planned.* With the swiftness of a cheetah, his fingers traveled to her core and moved her lace panties aside. She prepared herself for him to push his fingers inside her core, but instead he played with her lips before rubbing his thumb over her clit.

Her hips rose off the boxes, only to be gently coaxed back down by Jaleen. Just like his kisses, he took his time exploring her core, maintaining eye contact the entire time he did so. Usually she hated maintaining eye contact when she was doing anything intimate. However, Jaleen's gaze was so erotic that she literally could not look anywhere else besides deep into his eyes. He increased the motion of his thumb and slipped two fingers into her core. Slowly he worked his fingers in a nice rhythm that could only be described as the beginning cords of a smooth R & B ballad.

The more his fingers played with her insides, the harder it was to maintain eye contact. She dropped her head back when he increased his rhythm.

"You're breathtaking," he whispered before placing soft kisses along her neck and collarbone. Her thighs opened wider, the fabric more constricting than she wanted it to be. He must have sensed her urgency to move her skirt out of the way because he expertly lifted her off the boxes to push her skirt above her waist before continuing his objective of pleasing her in ways she hadn't imagined.

He fell to his knees and placed her legs on either side of his shoulders, dropping provocative kisses along her thighs. Instead of removing his fingers like she assumed he was going to, he kept them buried deep inside her and ran his tongue along the same places his hands had already explored.

I should have known it would feel like this. She should have known that there was no way it wouldn't be this explosive between them. No way could she tell him about her desire to be thoroughly kissed and think that Jaleen wouldn't take on the challenge. Jaleen was all about challenges. She'd watched him dare others to underestimate his abilities so that he could prove them wrong. He hadn't become as successful as he was by doing anything mediocre and the way his tongue was dipping deep within her, exploring places that had otherwise been left untouched for entirely too long, was his way of confirming that her expectations hadn't been set too high. If anything, they'd been set too low because what Jaleen was doing to her didn't compare to her fantasies. It surpassed them.

Her orgasm approached quicker than she'd realized. She opened her mouth to warn Jaleen and wasn't sure if she made sense. From the squeaks she heard in the room, she'd hoped she'd gotten at least one legible word out, but instead of slowing the onslaught of his mouth, he only increased the pressure.

She'd once overheard a couple of women talking in a café about experiencing the type of orgasms that made a woman forget where she was and what time it was. The kind that had her questioning backward from forward and left from right. The kind that had a woman forgetting her entire name…first, last and middle. That conversation was the only thing Danni could think of to describe the explosive orgasm she experienced as a result of the expert hands and mouth of Jaleen Walker. Now she knew why all the women in Chicago had been bending over backward to go on a date with him. Being on the receiving end of a man like Jaleen wasn't just a chapter to add to your memories. It was the entire damn book.

Chapter 8

Jaleen glanced inside the restaurant at Danni who was enthusiastically talking to Christian Serrano and his manager. They'd just arrived in Barcelona that morning, two hours before Danni had scheduled the meeting. They hadn't even checked into the hotel yet, which left Jaleen sitting with their luggage at a table outside of the vintage restaurant.

"Here is your food, sir."

"Thank you," Jaleen said to the waitress with the beautiful Spanish accent. He didn't know much about fashion, but Danni had informed him on the plane that Christian's family owned the restaurant. It was rich in history and recipes passed down from generation to generation. Jaleen really hoped the meeting was going well because carrying Serrano's swimsuit designs in the Bare Sophistication boutiques would be a huge opportunity for Danni and the Dupree sisters.

After spending Friday night locked in a storage room with Danni, he'd been disappointed when Autumn showed up twenty minutes after the most erotic experience of his life. When they'd gone back to his place, Danni had teased him about that night being the best unplanned second date she'd ever had. In hindsight, it was the best date he'd ever had, too.

He'd had every intention to continue the night with Danni when he'd received an urgent phone call from his cousin Jasper who was still in Europe. After two hours of working out an issue with a property overseas, he'd gone to check on Danni only to find she'd fallen asleep. As much as he'd wanted to wake her, she'd needed her sleep, so instead he'd lay next to her on the couch until he'd fallen asleep, too.

Sleeping with a woman for comfort instead of sex was entirely new to him, but he welcomed the feeling. Danni wasn't just sexy as hell. She oozed sex appeal more than any woman he'd ever met in his entire life. He'd dated a range of women, including an award-winning actress, an up-and-coming reality star, a gorgeous plus-size model, a famous chef—and no, not Artemela Rojas—he'd even dated a well-known politician. However, none of those women even came close to making him feel what he was beginning to feel with Danni.

If he thought back to the first time he'd met her, he realized that he'd always known she'd be different. He'd always known that the minute he tasted her, he'd want more. He'd want something deeper with her. He'd desire what he deemed impossible. In his situation, he couldn't afford to fall in love with someone he cared about the way he cared about her. Not only did it spell trouble for him, but he feared the damage it would do to her would be irreparable.

His phone rang, interrupting his thoughts and meal. *It's Taheim...* He had a feeling his friend was calling about Danni and contemplated not answering, even if he did have an international phone plan.

"What's up, Taheim?"

"Not much, man. I just called because I heard you were in Chicago for a day and now you're in Barcelona..."

"Yeah. Sorry I couldn't hit you up while I was there, but I had meetings with my family all Friday."

"I heard," Taheim said. "Winter mentioned that you flew down here with Danni and that she went to work at the shop while you went to your meetings. Then you guys got locked in the storage room?"

"Sure did," Jaleen said with a laugh. "I accidently locked us in there, but it was only for, like, three hours or so."

"What's going on with you two?"

As his best friend, Jaleen knew that tone in Taheim's voice. Taheim wasn't really one to ask him any questions about the women he hung out with, so Taheim was fishing for information.

"We've been hanging out together a lot lately, so I asked her if she wanted to come back to Chicago with me for the weekend. She needed to go to Barelona for an impromptu meeting and asked if I'd join her since I've been here a couple times. That's all."

"Are you sure that's all?"

Jaleen took a sip of water before responding. "Why don't you tell me the real reason you called?"

"You know why I called," Taheim said, sterner than before. "Jay, what are you doing, man? Danni's like family to Winter, Autumn and Summer. She's a part of our group of friends."

"Meaning?"

"Meaning you can't date her then discard her like you do all those other women."

"This coming from the man who used to be my partner in crime," Jaleen said. "Let's not forget that you used to be just like me, but you changed. You went from having eyes for multiple women to only having eyes for one. Why is it so hard to believe that I won't treat Danni like I do those other women?" His voice was rising, but he didn't care.

"That's not what I'm saying and you know it." Taheim sighed. "Look, I know you well enough to know that you've always felt differently about Danni. Hell, anyone who hangs out with you two for any amount of time can see the chemistry. But my guess is that you aren't frustrated that I called to ask you about your intentions. You're frustrated because you've probably already been asking yourself the same questions. I'm the only one who knows why you can't fall for Danni, so I'm assuming you knew this call was coming but are pissed all the same."

Jaleen let out a frustrated breath as he let Taheim's words sink in. "You're right," he finally said. "All of it. You're right. But, man, I don't know what it is. I know that I should stay away from her. I know I'm no good for her. And I know in the end we will both end up hurt. But I can't help myself. When I'm not with her, all I do is think about her. At this point, I'm not sure I could stay away if I tried."

"I know the feeling," Taheim said. "What's going to happen in a few months when you turn thirty-five? What will you do then?"

"I've been thinking about that, but I'm not liking any option I come up with. When the time comes, I guess I'll follow my obligations, but I damn sure won't like it."

"Then maybe you should tell her," he suggested. "Maybe you should tell her the real reason why your relationship can't last long."

Jaleen didn't want to sound vulnerable, but he couldn't help feeling that way when he thought about Danni. "What if she decides she doesn't want to talk to me again? What if she doesn't understand that a marriage based off love is not in my future?"

"Telling her will be the most difficult conversation you've ever had. But she deserves to know the truth," Taheim said. "And who knows…she may surprise you."

He highly doubted that, but Taheim was right. She did deserve to know the truth. Deep down, he knew he and Danni couldn't go on like this. What would happen if he and Danni did fall in love and then he had to let her go? What would they do if they started developing strong feelings for one another?

He could be lost in thought for hours if he let the questions he had about his relationship with Danni cloud his mind. Hell, in some ways they already were. However, despite the fact that he could cut off some of his worry by only living in the moment and not thinking about the future, there was one main thought that continued to float around in his mind, setting up a permanent place in his psyche. *Maybe you've already fallen too hard.*

A few hours after her meeting with Christian Serrano, Danni was still elated that she'd landed one of the most sought after swimsuit designers for Bare Sophistication.

They still had to work out the contract, but she'd been impressed by Christian and his manager. It was obvious that Christian not only valued his work, but also understood what it meant for the Serrano name. Now, she knew why Bare Sophistication and other smaller boutiques appealed to Christian. He was from humble beginnings and was very family oriented. An hour into their meeting, she'd had the pleasure of meeting his parents, two sisters, and two brothers who had made an appearance.

Jaleen had eventually joined in on the fun and once the Serrano's learned that Danni and Jaleen were residing at a quaint resort-villa in a coastal town just outside of Barcelona, Mr. Serrano had recommended an oceanfront restaurant in the area.

Being the gentleman he was, Jaleen had invited Christian and his manager the join them for dinner. The gesture had really impressed Danni because she sensed he'd rather spend the only night they had in Barcelona dining alone.

They were scheduled to meet their dining companions in an hour and a half, however, Jaleen had just phoned her to ask that she be ready in thirty minutes. After putting on her lilac maxi dress, fluffing her wavy hair, and applying a little makeup, she was ready to go.

Danni glanced at the clock on the nightstand by the bed. "Hmm, I still have ten minutes to spare," she said to herself.

They were staying in a two-bedroom villa, so Jaleen was right down the hall. Although Danni figured he was probably ready as well, she decided to take some time to think about everything that had happened over the last few days.

Opening the sliding door to the balcony, Danni sank into the plush cushion on the wicker outdoor chair and placed her cell phone on the round, glass table. The ocean was beautiful and calming, offering the piece of tranquillity that she needed.

To say that her time with Jaleen in Chicago had been uneventful would be a huge understatement. She'd expected to enjoy the time she'd spent with him, but she hadn't expected to enjoy their time together as much as she had.

And he knows about my list. They never got the opportunity to discuss how much he actually knew about her "Thirty Things To Do Before I'm Thirty" list, but she assumed she'd said enough for him to know he was on it. He obviously knew that kissing him had been on the list.

She'd thought about bringing it up on the plane ride to Barcelona, but she'd been so nervous about her meeting with Christian Serrano that she'd spent most the time preparing.

Just thinking about the time she'd spent in the storage room with Jaleen sent desire spiraling through her entire body. She couldn't have prepared herself for what had happened, but she didn't regret a moment they'd spent trapped in that room. Unfortunately getting trapped in the storage room hadn't been the only unexpected thing to happen in Chicago. She hadn't anticipated the call she'd received on her way to Bare Sophistication, however, looking back, she probably should have been prepared for the call.

It had been almost four years since she'd made one of the worst decisions of her life and almost two years that she'd been paying someone to keep her secret. When she'd initially moved to Chicago from Tampa, it had been easy to ignore the decisions she'd made. Now it seemed like her past mistakes were coming back to bite her in the butt and her biggest fear was that someone she cared about would get hurt in the process.

Her mind drifted to her mother. Whenever she was overwhelmed with thoughts, her mom was the only person in the world who could calm her down. She picked her cell phone up and checked the time zone for Florida before she dialed her number.

"Hi, Mom," Danni said. "I hope I didn't interrupt you."

"Oh, no, sweetie, I wasn't doing anything important. Why did you call me through FaceTime audio?"

Shoot! Danni didn't have an international calling package, so she'd tapped into the hotel's Wi-Fi. She was glad her iPhone allowed you to call with a Wi-Fi signal, but she didn't want her mom to know she was in Barcelona. Any time she went out of the country, all her mom did was worry. She wanted to tell her mother about Christian Serrano, but she'd mention that after the contract was finalized.

"No reason. I was just thinking about you and wanted to give you a call."

"Are you okay, Danni? I get the feeling something is going on."

More like so much is going on I don't even know where to start. Danni would be the first to admit that her mom was one of her best friends. There was nothing she couldn't share with her and, oftentimes, her mother knew her better than she knew herself.

"Well, I'm glad you called," Regina said after Danni remained silent. "You can tell me what's wrong when you're ready. In the meantime, how about you tell me more about this young man you started dating. Unless he's the reason something is wrong."

"What makes you think I'm dating someone?"

"Let's just call it a mother's intuition. Or maybe it's possible that I called your job when you didn't answer my call yesterday and was informed that you weren't in the office."

Danni laughed. "And why would you think that means I'm dating someone?"

"Well, I remember calling your job last month when you hadn't answered your phone and you were driving back from visiting me in Tampa. I had wanted to make sure you'd arrived. Summer informed me that you hadn't arrived yet, but was excited to tell me all about how well your celebration dinner went. Including the fact that one of your friends, Jaleen, was in town for the dinner."

"He wasn't in town for the dinner. He's in town for work."

"Ah, so he's still in town? He's the young man from Chicago, right? The one you once told me you couldn't stand then proceeded to complain about him during your entire weekend visiting me?"

"Um, yeah, that's him. But I still don't understand what

he has to do with the fact that you assumed I was dating someone."

"Oh, come on, I wasn't born yesterday. You've randomly worked him into our conversations for years."

Seriously? How could I not have noticed that? "That's because we share so many mutual friends. Besides, we aren't dating."

"Oh, okay. Guess I was wrong. How are things at the store?"

"Everything has been awesome. Sales are the highest we've seen them since we opened and Nicole and Aaliyah are killing it with the boudoir studio. We're still booked well into next year."

"Oh, honey, that's great to hear. Your brothers were just asking me about the boutique and the studio."

"Aw, how are they doing?"

"They are both doing fine. They promised to try to visit this Thanksgiving or Christmas, but you know how your brothers are. Always traveling from place to place. I'll believe it when I see it."

"Mom, are you sure you don't need me to visit more? I can increase my visits to twice a month instead of once a month now that I'm within driving distance."

After Danni's father, Derek, passed away five years ago, Danni had sworn she'd never leave Tampa since both her younger and older brother had already left home. However, circumstances had caused her to break that promise and because she had an amazing mom, Regina had been nothing but encouraging when she'd learned that Danni wanted to move to Chicago.

"Oh, I'm fine, Danni. I'm glad I get to see my baby girl every month, and I know I will see my boys soon, but don't put that pressure on yourself. I've joined enough organizations to keep myself busy."

"How could I forget? I think you introduced me to about three different groups of people that you hang out with during my last visit. Your social life is more active than mine."

"Speaking of social life, maybe you should ask Jaleen out on a date to help get his mind off work. I hear women asking men out is all the rage right now."

"I'll keep that in mind," Danni said with a laugh. "He has been pretty stressed since he's arrived in Miami. I think the project he's working on is more difficult than he'd anticipated and, since it's a family business, his family isn't making matters any easier."

"Sounds like a difficult situation. I know he's not your most favorite person, but I hope you've been supportive."

"I have been." Danni took another sip of her tea. "And he isn't that bad. We've managed to get along while he's been in Miami." *Understatement of the year.* Since the storage room was definitely a memorable experience, they'd still counted it as their second date. They still had to plan a third date.

"So he isn't as bad as you thought?"

Danni thought about all the time they'd spent together so far. Needless to say, she couldn't find anything she disliked about Jaleen *except* the fact that maybe she liked him too much. "No, he isn't as bad as I thought. We're developing an actual friendship."

"Friendship, huh? Well, I'm glad to hear that." They discussed a few more things before wrapping up their call.

"Oh, and before I forget," Regina said. "Make sure you tell Jaleen hello for me when you go out to dinner tonight."

Danni almost dropped the phone. "Dinner? What dinner?"

"Are we still playing this game?" Regina asked. "Don't you have plans for dinner tonight?"

Danni racked her brain, trying to figure out how her mother knew she was with Jaleen in Barcelona.

"Mom, how did you know I was going to dinner with Jaleen?"

"I already told you. Mother's intuition."

"Seriously, Mom?"

"Well, maybe I sent him a message on Facebook and asked."

Danni's jaw dropped. "I thought you said you weren't really on Facebook?"

"I said I was occasionally on Facebook and an hour ago, I decided to send him a message."

"How did you even find him?"

"Duh, I went and searched through your friends list. Maybe you should have hidden your friends list if you didn't want me snooping. I requested to be his friend and he accepted me. That's when I asked him when your next date was and he mentioned that he was having dinner with you today."

"So you basically tricked him? He probably thought I'd mentioned him to you."

"You have. Several times in fact."

"You know what I mean. He thought I'd told you we were dating and that you just wanted clarification."

"Hmm, you could be right. Just like he clarified that you went to Chicago with him and were now in Barcelona."

"He told you that?" Danni asked, her voice a little higher than usual.

"No, but you just did." Regina's laugh filled her ears. "He posted two photos on his Facebook page. One of Grant Park in Chicago and another of a beach in Barcelona. I would ask why you didn't tell me you were in Barcelona, but I assume you knew I'd be worried with you being there alone. However, you aren't alone. You're with Jaleen."

Danni rubbed her forehead. Whenever she forgot how observant her mom was, her mother would do something to remind her. "Okay, Mom. I think I've had enough trickery for one phone call. It's dinnertime in Barcelona, so I should probably hang up and meet Jaleen."

"I understand, sweetie. Call me when you get back to the United States. I can't wait to hear how you ended up traveling with this man you claim you don't like. I checked out his pictures, too, and he's a real cutie."

"Who are you?" Danni said, shaking her head. "I'm hanging up now." Danni ended the call with her mom, still reeling over everything her mother had figured out.

"Obviously anyone who calls me Sherlock Danni has never met my mom," Danni said to herself. Just as she went back inside, there was a knock at her door. She grabbed her purse before she opened the door. Her steps almost faltered at how handsome he looked. He was wearing beige slacks and a sea-blue shirt that really made his complexion pop.

"You look beautiful," Jaleen said as he looked her up and down. The look he was giving her alone sent tingles running through her body.

"You look handsome, as well," Danni said before closing her room door. "So why did you want to meet early?"

"I figured this was the only alone time we'd get." Jaleen held open the main door so that Danni could walk through first. The minute they both stepped outside, they were welcomed by a warm breeze. "I thought walking along the beach may be nice. It's only about a mile or so away."

The sun was setting, turning the sky a brilliant reddish-orange and casting a vibrant glow across the ocean.

"A nice walk sounds perfect."

Jaleen removed his loafers while Danni removed her wedges as soon as they reached the sand. For the first couple of minutes, they walked in comfortable silence.

"Do you remember when we first met?" Danni asked, breaking the silence.

"When I made you that drink at the bar and you turned me down?"

She glanced at Jaleen, unsure if she should jog his memory. "Um, I'm actually thinking about a time before that. A few days before to be exact. I guess we officially met at the bar, but we had crossed paths before then."

Jaleen looked at her questionably. "Okay, so when did this unofficial meeting take place?"

You vowed you'd never bring up this moment. Yet here she was, bringing it up.

"News was traveling fast about the Bare Sophistication masquerade lingerie parties and Winter and I had just finished our third party in a week. That particular night, we were in the Gold Coast area and it was going on two a.m."

She studied his eyes to see if recognition dawned and continued when he still looked confused.

"The party had just ended and I was exhausted. The bride to be was a bridezilla so I decided to take a short break by sitting in the stairwell since I figured most the attendees would be taking the elevator, and Winter was catering to the models. I had unintentionally began nodding off when you almost tripped over me."

"You're kidding me," Jaleen said. "You were the masked woman in the stairwell who cursed me out?"

"You're damn right I cursed you out," she said with a laugh. "You could have hurt me because you were too busy trying to tuck your shirt in your pants after leaving your booty call's place that night."

"I'll have you know that Trisha was not a booty call and I was there because she'd needed a friend to talk to after a long workweek."

Danni stopped walking and crossed her arms over her

chest. "Save the lies for someone who doesn't know you as well as I do. Besides, you admitted that it was a booty call that night."

"Oh," Jaleen said sheepishly. "Well, I'm sure I only admitted that because you were trying to pick a fight with me. And why were you wearing a mask if you were hosting the party?"

"We always wear costumes when we host a party," Danni said. "It's adds to the ambiance."

"So you knew who I was when I flirted with you a few days after at the bar?"

"Of course I remembered you," Danni said. "It's not every night I meet a man who almost trips over me, then proceeds to tell me I killed his happy vibe. Before he gives me a big smile, probably while thinking about the woman whose apartment he just left."

"Man," Jaleen said with a laugh. "I had no idea it was you. But I should have known that feisty stairwell beauty was none other than Danni Allison. You wanted to argue that night and any time we bicker, it's because you start it."

"I'm pretty sure you're the one who starts most of our fights."

"Not true," Jaleen said. "You're the one who is always claiming that I like to hear myself talk—"

"Which is completely true."

"Even so, you like to talk, too, so that makes us even. And you're always claiming that I joke too much—"

"Which you do and I have people who would cosign that fact."

Jaleen snapped his fingers. "What about the fact that you call me a player all the time?"

Danni rolled her eyes. "Oh, come on, you and I both know that you'll date anything with a pulse. And I just reminded you about the first night we met. I'm surprised you even remember Trisha's name."

Jaleen placed his arms over his chest. "I'm offended. Need I remind you that this so-called *player* managed to have you eating out of the palm of his hand in the storage room?"

Danni gasped. "Of course you would see it that way!"

Jaleen popped his collar. "I mean, I know I'm sexy, but you didn't have to spill your dirty kissing secrets to get me to kiss you in the storage room. I would have done that free of charge."

Before she could second-guess what she was doing, she was chasing him down the beach not caring that they were headed to dinner in a few and she needed to look presentable.

She was a fast runner but apparently not fast enough to catch up to Jaleen. When she stopped to catch her breath, he stopped and walked over to her.

"There's a bench over there," Jaleen said between pants. "Want to sit for a few minutes?"

"Sure," she said before following him. Once they sat, she glanced over at him. His eyes were dancing with amusement that she assumed mirrored hers. They both broke out in laughter at the same time.

"Man, I needed that laugh," Jaleen said. "It's been a rough few months."

It wasn't what he said that made her take notice, but the way he said it.

"I'm sorry that you've been having such a hard time at Walker Partner Realty," she said. "Must be difficult to work with family and have a difference of opinion."

"You can say that again," Jaleen said as he placed his arm behind her on the bench. "My family has a long line of traditions that are not to be broken. Some of those traditions are life changing."

"How life changing?"

"Well, my father is the oldest of five sons, however, my uncle Jake is the only brother who works for Walker Partner Realty. One of my uncles is a politician, another is a lawyer and the youngest is a doctor."

"Hold on a second. Is former Senator Jeffrey Walker your uncle?" Danni didn't follow politics, but she knew enough.

"One and the same. But, no matter what career a Walker has, one thing remains the same. Business always comes first. Not family. Not love. Business."

"Seems harsh."

"It is, but for my family, following a certain set of rules is expected. As close as I was to my grandfather, he also believed in making certain business decisions that would benefit the family both financially and in social standing. In my family's mind, every Walker must appease to certain obligations by the time they reach thirty years of age. Guess you can call me special because I got an extra five years before I have to accept my destiny."

The crease in his forehead had been present the moment he began discussing his family. As the waves gently brushed on shore, she studied the man who intrigued her more every day. Judging by the way he described his family, they couldn't be more different.

"What is your destiny?" she asked.

"Can I ask you a question instead?"

She shrugged. "Sure. Ask me whatever you want."

He studied her eyes. "Have you ever wanted something so bad, that you feared by going after what you wanted, you'd hurt a lot of people in the process."

"Of course I have. I think everyone goes through some form of similar struggle in their lives."

"I agree. But the difficult part for me has always been the aftermath. What happens after I make a decision that I can't take back. At what point does going after what you want constitute as being selfish if you blatantly disregard the feelings of others in the process?"

"The same can be said for not going after what you want," Danni said. "Others will always have an opinion on what they think is best for you, but it's your prerogative to be your own judge of character, as well."

"Trust me. I've spent my entire life trying to live life by my own set of rules, while still maintaining the traditions and values I was raised with. Sometimes, it's difficult to appease all parties involved when fate may have already played its cards."

"Is what's deemed as your destiny the reason you won't go after what you really want?"

"Yes," he said staring out into the ocean. "It is."

"And what is it that you want?"

Danni felt as if Jaleen's head turned in slow motion as her heart skipped a beat, awaiting his answer.

"I'm looking at exactly what I want." His penetrating stare held her hostage. "And sometimes, I even allow myself to dream that I can have it."

You can have it! Danni wanted to yell it at the top of her lungs, but his next words gave her pause.

"In this case, the problem with getting what I want means that I would hurt you the most. And I could never allow that to happen."

"Why?" she asked, her voice so low she barely recognized herself. "Why would I be the most hurt?"

"Because I'm a Walker," Jaleen said in a serious tone.

"And being a Walker means business will always come first. Not family. Not love—"

"Business," Danni finished.

She knew what Jaleen was trying to do. He was trying to warn her that he wasn't the type of man she should fall for. She wondered if he realized that he was guilty of exactly what he claimed he didn't like. He was trying to decide their fate without even giving her the option of proving him wrong.

Chapter 9

Danni hated to admit it, but even though she'd just seen Jaleen three days ago, she really missed him. Although she'd enjoyed their extended weekend in Chicago and Barcelona, the trip had been filled with more business than pleasure.

When they'd arrived back to Miami, they had agreed on a date tonight. She was just finishing her yoga routine when her doorbell rang. *Who could that be?* When she looked through her peephole, she gasped at the face staring back at her. She glanced at her Fitbit, noticing that it was four hours before her date with Jaleen.

"I'm sorry, did I misinterpret the time our date was supposed to begin?" Instead of responding to her, Jaleen leaned in for a quick kiss that was entirely too short for Danni's liking.

"May I come in?"

"Of course." She stepped aside to let him in.

"No, you didn't misinterpret anything. I needed to pick your brain before our next date. I should have talked to you earlier."

"How did you know I was home?"

"I went to the boutique first and Summer mentioned that you were off today."

"Oh, okay. What did you need to talk to me about?"

"About your list. The one that included things you wanted to do before your birthday."

"Aha, so I did mention what type of list it was to you."

"Not exactly. You only mentioned it was a 'Thirty Things To Do Before You're Thirty' list and then you mentioned that I was on it…more than once."

She walked over to her yoga mat and began rolling it up. She was well aware of Jaleen's eyes trained to her movements. "Any chance you can forget everything I said that night?"

"Not a chance," he said with a laugh. "I learned some valuable information that night. Had you never gotten tipsy, we may have never had the opportunity to get to know one another better. Or in the storage room." He suggestively raised his eyebrows.

"Humph. Someone's cocky tonight."

"Baby, I'm always cocky." He strutted around her living room. "Didn't you get the memo?"

He was feeling good. She'd missed this side of him. The playful side that didn't seem to have a care in the world. Their conversation in Barcelona had taken a serious turn when they'd walked along the beach. Even so, she needed to remind him who was in charge. She put her mat aside, purposely bending over more than she needed to. She'd just ordered the pink-and-teal yoga pants and sports bra set she was wearing. Even her simple pink tank was new.

"If you keep distracting me with that luscious behind, I won't be able to remember what I came here for."

"I think it had something to do with our date tonight and my prebirthday list."

"Oh, right," he said, snapping his fingers. "Let's start with what's on the list. Care to share it with me?"

She was already shaking her head before he finished his sentence. "In the words you so eloquently told me, not a chance."

"Why not?"

"Well, for starters, it's a private list." She sat on her sofa. "And secondly, no one knows about the list, so had I not been tipsy, you wouldn't have found out about it, either."

There were so many more reasons why she couldn't share the list, but she didn't want to dive into details. There were some key bullet points that revealed entirely too much about herself. Secrets that would no doubt alter the course of their relationship.

"What's going on in that beautiful head of yours?"

Danni glanced toward Jaleen who was still standing near the wall. He was wearing dark gray jogging pants and a fitted white tee. His sunglasses were pushed on top of his head and, judging by the hot look he was shooting her way, he should have been wearing those shades to block his piercing stare. "Too much is swarming in my head for me to put into words." She picked up her glass of water from the coffee table and took a sip. "Do you want anything to drink?"

"What have you got?"

"Water, wine and hot or iced tea."

"Is it your infamous iced tea recipe?" he asked. "The one you usually make for the parties?"

She took another sip of water. "One and the same."

"Then I'll have that."

Danni welcomed the cool air that teased her face when she opened the refrigerator. She would have taken more advantage of her trip to the kitchen had her kitchen and living room not been connected with an open floor plan.

She still felt his eyes on her although he'd now made his way to the same sofa she'd been sitting on.

"Here you go," she said, handing him the glass. She took a seat on the spot she'd previously vacated.

"Thank you." He watched her over the glass as he took a swig. She wasn't the only one with a lot on her mind. She could read the questions in his eyes. Questions that all seemed to center around her list and what was on it.

"I accomplished twenty-two goals I put on my list, but the last eight are a little harder to achieve."

He looked at her expectantly, waiting for her to continue.
You want to share a few things with him.

She shook her head at the thought, knowing all too well that it was true. She'd never met anyone she wanted to share private things about her life with, but Jaleen was one of those people.

"I guess I can tell you about a few things left on my list." She fidgeted with her fingers. "The last item is something I absolutely cannot share with you. It's too personal. Too close to my heart. But for the others..." She looked into his eyes. "I trust you."

She expected to see relief in his eyes, but instead she saw warning. "Don't put too much trust in me, Danni." He placed his glass on the table. "I promise that I will cherish what you share and I will try my best to see if I can help you knock off a few items on your list."

Don't trust him? She heard his words but she was having a hard time believing they were true. So far, he hadn't done anything to break her trust and a part of her wondered if his warning tonight, as well as his warning in Barcelona, was more of a defense mechanism. A way to keep him from getting too invested in a woman. She also wondered if he knew how invested he already appeared to be.

Based on the way she was feeling, it was hard to believe that her feelings were only one-sided.

She scooted closer to him on the sofa. "Close your eyes," she whispered. "And no peeking." When she was convinced he couldn't see her, she went to her bookcase and pulled out her favorite book. In the back on the binding sat her list. A list she kept close to her heart.

"You have to promise me that you will never try to see the list."

"Okay, I promise," Jaleen said. "I'll only see what you show me."

"Deal, you can open your eyes."

His eyes went straight to the paper in her hands. "You're trembling."

"Sorry," she said, straightening her spine. "I guess I'm a little nervous." She glanced at the list. *You're not ready,* she thought. *You're not ready to show him the entire list.* "How about I read a few to you?"

"Sounds good." Jaleen turned so that he was faced more toward her. "I'm ready when you are."

She opened the paper slowly, her eyes darting from the sheet to him. "I guess I should start by saying that you've already helped me cross off three things on my list. One item was sneaking into a movie and seeing two movies while only paying for one. It seems childish, but I'd never done something like that...until our first date."

He smiled, but his eyes urged her to continue. "Another item that you helped me accomplish was experiencing a thoroughly good kiss. The type of toe-curling kiss that made me forget about any and everything going on in the world around me." A shiver ran through her body at the thought of just how erotic their first kiss had been. Way more than she'd anticipated when she'd placed that item on the list.

"And another item on the list that you helped make happen," she said as she cleared her throat, "was to have an orgasm with all of my clothes on. So yeah, you were…um, we accomplished that in the storage room, too."

Pull it together.

"Another item on my list is to skydive at night. I can't even imagine the thrill from doing something like that."

She wasn't the type to get nervous, but Jaleen wasn't showing any emotion as he listened to her read the items he'd helped her accomplish and items she hadn't yet accomplished. His silence should have made her take pause and keep the next item private, but she didn't want to. She was well aware that there were more sexual bullet points left on her list than anything else. When she'd been concocting the list, it hadn't mattered since she'd known she was the only person who'd ever read the list. She'd wanted to be honest with herself about the things she wanted to accomplish in the course of a year and, surprisingly, some of those things were sexual.

"One of the items I still have left that I'm sure I won't accomplish, but placed on the list anyway, was to have an…was to experience a…was to—"

Are you baiting him?

She already knew he accepted challenges. Was she proposing her next aspiration as one she feared wouldn't happen so that he could prove her wrong?

"One item is that I want to have an intimate experience in a public place," she blurted. "With the possibility that someone else could walk in on the erotic act happening." *There, I said it.* She gazed into his eyes, expecting to see anything but a cool and calm facade. However, that's exactly what she got. *How did that not faze him? Nada! Zilch!*

"Anyway, I'll continue." She scrolled the list to see what else she was willing to read when he finally spoke.

"Can I interrupt you for a second?"

"Sure. What is it?"

His eyes studied hers, briefly dropping to her lips as he spoke. "Of the twenty-two things you'd already accomplished, how many of those items were intimate or sexual ambitions?"

"Only two," she answered honestly.

"The two I've already been a part of?"

More like a leading man, but tomato, tomahto. "Yes."

He studied her some more. "How many of the eight that you have left are intimate or sexual ambitions?"

"Including the one I just mentioned," she said, glancing at her list. "Three of the eight that are left."

His jaw clenched, the only movement he'd given her since they'd began discussing the list. "So when you were creating this list, who did you have in mind to help you accomplish all five of your sexual goals? Or did you not have a particular man in mind?"

She didn't respond right away but instead let his words play around in her mind. Deep down, she already knew the answer. She'd always been a visual person and looking back on the time she'd created the list, there'd been only one man she'd visualized. One man who inspired desires in her that had been dormant for way too long. She had no clue what was brewing between her and Jaleen, but she did know that she needed to experience more with him.

"Do you want to know why I agreed to your bet last month?" she asked. "Why I didn't debate your suggestion when you laid out the rules?"

He focused on her lips again. "I have an idea and I'm hoping like hell that I'm right."

Danni looked him in the eye, refusing to look away. "It's because there was only one man who I knew would bring me the type of pleasure that I desire. So if you're asking if I imagined you being the man to satisfy me in ways I'd always craved more than I'd cared to admit, then the answer is yes. I didn't have just any man in mind. I had you in mind for each and every aspiration."

Her words seemed to pierce straight through him and break the resolve he'd been holding on to since he'd walked through her door. He pulled her to him until she had no choice but to straddle him.

"Since our date isn't for a few more hours, I was trying to be on my best behavior with you," he said as he placed kisses along her collarbone, trailing his tongue over the tops of her breasts concealed by her sports bra and tank top.

"I never asked you to be on your best behavior," Danni said as she started rolling her hips over his hardening shaft. When their lips finally met, his tongue stoked hers in languid movements, causing her to moan in satisfaction at the slow, seductive dance. The sensational feeling was almost too much. She didn't know what he had for planned tonight, but wasn't sure she could wait. She was already sexually charged and it would be so easy to remove their clothes right now and continue what they'd started in the storage room. Jaleen seemed to be on the same page as she was. Unfortunately his employees hadn't gotten the memo.

Whoever was calling his phone called three times before Jaleen finally broke their kiss to answer it.

"I'm so sorry," he said before answering. "This is Jaleen."

Danni couldn't hear the caller on the other end of the line, but she didn't need to know who it was to see that the call was one he didn't want to have. He ended the call a few minutes later.

"I can't believe I'm saying this, but I have to get back to work. We'll continue this tonight, okay?"

"Okay," she said, leaning in for one more kiss. As with their previous kiss, it escalated within seconds.

"If I don't get out of here, I might be out of a job," he said with a laugh.

As she led him to the door, he pulled her in for one more quick kiss. "Tonight, wear something comfortable. Similar to what you have on now. Bring a pair of workout shorts with you, too. I'll be back to pick you up in three hours."

I'd rather not have to wear clothes at all. "Okay," she said instead as she closed the door behind him. She lightly touched her lips and plopped onto the sofa. If anyone had told her that, eventually, she'd be sharing passionate kisses with Jaleen, she wasn't sure she'd have believed them. But that's exactly what was happening. She glanced at the piece of paper folded on her coffee table. A piece of paper that contained a secret on a list that couldn't afford to be read.

Be careful, Danni, her inner voice warned. *There's a reason you didn't want to get close to him. Don't forget that he's not the only one worried about you finding out too much about him. He can't find out too much about you, either.*

Danni swatted the air as if her thoughts were a fly she wanted to smack down. She had a date to prepare for and worrying about the secrets she kept buried inside wasn't exactly the way she wanted to kick off the night.

Chapter 10

"Where exactly are you taking me?" Danni asked. Jaleen had blindfolded her because he hadn't wanted her to see where they were going. He'd only been to this part of town a couple of times, but he'd checked out the venue the night before to make sure he knew his way.

"We're here," he said as he parked in a back lot and removed her blindfold. Danni looked around the empty lot near a darkened alley.

"Okay, when you said I was in for an intriguing date, none of what I'd fantasized included dark alleys and shady parking lots."

Jaleen laughed as he got out of the car and opened her door. "Maybe you'll feel differently when we head inside." He led her to a door with a security guard standing outside.

"Tickets," the guard said, shining a flashlight in their faces. Jaleen showed him their tickets.

"When you enter, go down the stairs on the left. Then make a quick right. Walk down the long hall and enter the doors that say Pearl Harmony. You'll get further instructions when you arrive."

"Okay, now I'm intrigued," Danni whispered as they

followed the guard's directions. When they arrived at Pearl Harmony, a tiny, petite woman was there to greet them.

"Welcome to Pearl Harmony. I'll be your assistant, Mira. Have you been to Pearl Harmony before?"

"No, we haven't," Jaleen said.

"Then let me be the first to welcome you to your experience of a lifetime. Here at Pearl Harmony, we specialize in helping individuals achieve sexual pleasure through tantric practices including tantric massages and yoga."

Jaleen glanced at Danni just in time to see her eyes widen in surprise.

"While our tantric yoga and massages do not involve sexual intercourse," Mira continued, "they do involve complete sensual stimulation of the body. Tonight, you will be participating in our complete couples' package." Mira handed them two plastic bags. "Everything you will need is in the bags, including a pair of clothes that you can change into after your first session of the night. If you follow me, I will lead you to the changing rooms."

"Aren't you sneaky," Danni whispered to Jaleen as they followed Mira. "Tantric yoga? I never would have guessed this is what you had planned. Did you plan this after you saw me putting up my yoga mat earlier today?"

"Would you believe me if I told you I had this planned before I went to your place? And the fact that it mirrored something you were already semi-interested in was just a coincidence."

He was telling her the truth. He'd already had it planned, yet he was prepared to cancel his plans had he gone over her place today and sensed it was something she would be uncomfortable with. Instead, his visit had only increased his excitement for tonight.

"I believe you," she said.

"Are you okay with this? I don't want you to do anything that will make you uncomfortable."

"No, I'm willing to try it, especially since I knew that at least one of our dates would involve me having to wear minimal clothing." She playfully shoved his shoulder.

There's something else I bet you won't guess, either. Warning her of what was yet to come would be the gentlemanly thing to do. Good thing he didn't pride himself on being a gentleman.

"Here we are." Mira stopped in front of two sets of doors. "Women can change by going through this door and men can go through the other door. There are lockers available for you to place your personal belongings.

"When you picked up your tickets, you should have been informed that both women and men are to wear exercise shorts and women are to wear a sports bra. The clothing in the bag is for after your yoga session. Please lock everything away, especially your phones. You won't need any of that during your session.

"There will be signs with directions on how to get to the different rooms. Follow the signs that detail the way to the Rejuvenation room." Mira looked from one to the other. "I'll see you both on the other side."

It didn't take too long for Jaleen to change into a pair of black biking shorts and follow the necessary signs to meet Mira. Danni joined them a few minutes later wearing a baby blue sports bra and tight running shorts. *There's probably nothing this woman doesn't look good in.* Once together, they followed Mira into the room where three couples were already present.

"We only allow four couples to be in the room during this massage," Mira said in a low voice as she pointed to a large mat in the back of the room on the floor. "At the end of the massage, go back the way you came and meet me in the front Serenity room."

Once alone with the other couples, Jaleen and Danni followed suit and sat cross-legged like the other couples. The instructor entered the room shortly after.

"Ladies and gentlemen, my name is Hannah and I'll be your instructor this evening. As in most of my classes, I'd like to begin with a few simple breathing exercises."

Jaleen would never admit it to his boys, but tantric yoga was something he'd always been interested in but had never dared try.

After the breathing exercises, the instructor dimmed the lights even more and the music changed to an even more mellow tone.

"Okay, during my classes, I like to begin with a pose called Yab Yum. Gentlemen, if you would please turn to face your partners and continue to sit cross-legged on the mat." The men all did as told. "Ladies, now, you should sit on your partner's thighs and cross your ankles behind his back."

Danni slid onto Jaleen's lap with ease as they sat facing one another.

"Now, I want you to take the time and get comfortable in this position. Focus on the breathing exercises I just taught you. The goal of this pose is to align your energies and begin to breathe in harmony to deepen your connection. It's your choice if you'd rather keep your eyes open or closed."

Jaleen leisurely wrapped his arms around Danni's waist as she draped hers over his shoulders. Taking his cue from Danni, he kept his eyes open as they focused on their breathing while the instructor continued to speak.

"When you're in a relationship, no matter how old or new, it's important to make sure you're not only focusing on the physical attraction, but also on that person's soul. Now is the time for you to communicate without words. Leave your thoughts, hopes and wishes open for interpretation. Now is not the time to close yourself off, but rather, reach a new understanding that you never imagined you'd reach."

Jaleen let the instructor's words sink in as he maintained eye contact with Danni. He took note of things about her that he hadn't noticed before. He'd always thought her smooth mahogany skin tone was the type of rich, creamy color he'd never seen on anyone before. Uniquely hers, just like her round, dark ginger eyes that were the type of eyes a man could get lost in. However, tonight he also noticed how long and thick her eyelashes were. When she blinked, she slightly crinkled her nose, making his gaze focus on her lips. *Damn.* He really did love her pouty lips. He could also tell that she studied his facial features just as much.

Without even noticing when it had happened, their breathing began to match in unison and soon Jaleen found himself closing his eyes while leaning his forehead against hers.

I really needed this, he thought, trying to focus on the moment and push aside any thoughts about work. It was easy to do because, already, he could only feel her in his arms. He could only taste her on his lips after their earlier lip-lock. It was her natural fruity scent that was seeping into his nostrils, seducing him with promises of what they could be doing if there weren't others in the room.

Danni brought him a sense of comfort and support he hadn't felt in a long time…if ever. It was in the little things she did to show him that she genuinely cared about the struggles he may be dealing with. Whether it be placing her hand on his cheek or just doing things to help him overcome his thoughts if his mind ventured to topics he'd rather not think about, like they had when they'd initially been locked in the storage locker.

Even now, she was lightly rubbing her nose against certain parts of his face. He couldn't be certain, but he supposed that she could feel him clinging to her even if words weren't spoken. She could probably tell that she was his lifeline right now. She was the only person helping him get through this hellish time in his life that he still had yet to fully discuss with her.

"Okay," the instructor said after a few more moments. "I've asked my partner to join me to demonstrate the next five poses we will perform. We'll start with the dancer's pose."

Jaleen and Danni were the last to break the Yab Yum pose. If it were up to him, he would have stayed in that pose all night. The only reason he finally decided to let her go was the fact that he knew what was coming next... and he couldn't wait.

In the name of all that is holy, I don't think I'll ever forget tonight. Danni wasn't the type of person that had always loved yoga. It was definitely something she'd grown to love as she grew more intrigued by the science of yoga. Yet, tantric yoga was on a whole other level. She not only enjoyed the different poses that made her feel closer to Jaleen than she ever had before, but she also loved hearing about each description before they did the pose.

After yoga, she'd rinsed off and put on the shorts and shirt provided to her per Mira's instructions. Now, Mira had led her into a dimly lit room and handed her a note. When she asked if she should read it, Mira simply nodded. Danni unfolded the note and began to read it.

Dear Danni,

I hope you enjoyed tantric yoga as much as I did. The night isn't over yet. A woman as special as you are should always be treated like a queen. Based on our conversations, I get the feeling that men from your past haven't treated you as such. I aim to change that.

The future is uncertain, so I'd rather focus on the present. No matter how short or long our time together is, I want you to know that I'll cherish every moment I spend with you. There shouldn't be a day you doubt that you're a queen to me...in more ways than one.

I hope you enjoy this massage.
Sincerely,
Jay

There were so many parts of his letter that stood out, she didn't know where to start. First, she'd never had anyone treat her like a queen and Jaleen was making it extremely difficult to imagine any man living up to the standards he'd set. Second, he'd signed with his nickname *Jay*, not Jaleen. Only a few close to him called him Jay, so she felt honored that he'd addressed himself as such.

"You can keep on the shorts and shirt or you can undress to your comfort level," Mira said. "The massage bed is heated and extra cushions have been added per Mr. Walker's request. When you get under the top sheet, lie on your stomach. Your massage therapist will be in shortly."

"Thank you." As she slipped off her shirt and flip-flops, she wondered if Jaleen had hired an actual massage therapist or if he would be giving her a massage. If it were a stranger, she'd leave on her shorts. If not, she may be bold and remove all her clothing. She wasn't trying to be too forward, but she also wasn't sure how much longer she could handle the sexual tension between them without taking it another step forward, especially after such a stimulating yoga session.

Mind made up, she decided to completely undress. She'd just slipped under the sheet when there was a knock at the door.

"Come in." Although her head was down, she knew it was Jaleen. The room felt too energized for it not to be.

"Are you okay if I perform your massage?"

"Yes."

"Are you okay if I blindfold you?"

Oh, my goodness. What is he up to? "Yes, I'm fine with that."

"Just so you know, this is a tantric massage and yesterday I had a tutorial with a massage therapist to ensure I performed the proper techniques."

"Wow, you're really prepared."

"You have no idea." The timbre in his voice was so deep. So robust. Downright sexy. "Let's begin." He gently lifted her head so that he could blindfold her.

"I created a playlist. If it's too loud, let me know."

She hadn't noticed that music wasn't present in the room until smooth love songs began playing from a Bluetooth speaker.

"It's perfect."

The words had barely left her lips before he was already folding down the sheet, exposing her bare back. His hands started at her neck, massaging away what felt like weeks and months of stress. When he reached her back, she finally smelled the lavender aromatherapy oil he was using. His fingers slid up and down her spine, stopping right above the curve of her backside.

After about ten minutes she felt the sheet drop even farther, exposing her backside. She was so caught up in the moment that she couldn't make out the words he was mumbling under his breath. She didn't need clarification once he placed his hands on both cheeks and began massaging her butt. His fluid, circular strokes proved that he appreciated what she had to offer and damn if she could even focus on anything other than the pleasure he was giving her at the moment. She'd never had her butt massaged and once he removed the sheet completely and made his way to her thighs, she doubted any massage she had in the future would live up to a Jaleen Walker massage.

"In case I haven't told you enough, you are an extremely beautiful woman," he said, kneading her thighs with soft circles.

"Thank you." She almost stuttered the two simple words when he began caressing her feet. The feeling was indescribable.

"Can you turn over for me?"

She went to turn, and hesitated. *You'll be completely exposed if you turn over.* It wasn't that she was too shy to present herself in all her naked glory to Jaleen. It was the fact that she wouldn't be able to see his reaction because she was blindfolded.

"Don't worry, I'm lifting the sheet right now, so I can't see you."

She reached her hand behind her back and did, indeed, feel him holding the sheet up to block his view. The soft sheet covered her body after she'd turned. She expected him to start at her arms or shoulders, but instead she felt him pulling down the sheet over the swells of her breasts.

"Just relax," he said when she'd tensed. "Unless you want me to stop. If you do, just say the word."

"No, don't stop." Her voice sounded breathless to her ears. "I didn't tense because I want you to stop. I tensed in anticipation of what you'd planned to do next."

Even though she couldn't see his face, she imagined he was smiling at her response. Seconds later, her nipples perked when the cool air hit them. His hands began massaging her breasts, fingers twirling over her areolae. Her moans filled the room when he added another object to the mix. At first, she couldn't make out exactly what it was. When she realized it was an elongated feather, it only increased her pleasure.

Her breasts weren't the only place the feather explored. By the end of the massage, she didn't think there was a place on her body that the feather hadn't journeyed to.

"We're all done, beautiful." Jaleen said just as one of her favorite love songs was ending. "I hope you enjoyed it."

"It was amazing," she said, stretching out her oily body. "Thank you for that experience." She waited for his response, but was met with silence. When she pulled off her blindfold, she was in the room alone.

I didn't even hear him leave. As a matter of fact, she hadn't even technically laid eyes on him throughout the entire massage. She pulled the sheet closer to her chest just as there was a knock at the door.

"Come in." It was Mira.

"Mr. Walker told me to inform you that he will meet you in the Serenity room. I'll give you a moment to get dressed, then I'll take you to get your things."

After Mira shut the door, Danni leaned back on the table and quietly laughed to herself. "Leave it to Jaleen to leave me pining for more," she said out loud. It seemed to be a reoccurrence where he was concerned.

Chapter 11

Jaleen was hard as steel after the erotic massage he'd given Danni. Maintaining his self-control had been one of the toughest things he'd ever had to do. Now all that was left was executing the last part of his plan and hoping that Danni wasn't upset at the way he'd left after her massage.

He'd had every intention of taking the blindfold off her and making sure that she'd enjoyed everything, but he'd feared that if he'd stayed in that room even a minute longer, they'd have never left it.

He glanced around the empty locker room. *She should enter any minute now.* No longer had the thought left his mind, she entered the locker room looking more relaxed than he'd ever seen her look before. He'd covered her with a healthy amount of oil in hopes that she would want to rinse some of it off. Therefore, he was elated to see her make her way to the shower stalls.

Once she stepped into a stall and closed the curtain behind her, Jaleen walked over to the showers. He checked the locker room to make sure no one was around to see what he was doing before he stopped in front of the shower she was in.

He watched her arm peek out to drape her clothes over the side of the shower stall.

Okay, Walker. Now's the time to make your move.

He removed his shirt but hesitated when his hand went to the band of his shorts. *What if this isn't what she wants?* What had seemed like a good idea at first, suddenly seemed wrong. He usually never second-guessed if a woman wanted to take things to the next level. However, Danni wasn't just any woman. Besides, they hadn't really gotten a chance to talk much tonight. As much as he enjoyed the tantric couple's experience, talking hadn't been part of the equation. *Maybe I should just dip out before she sees or hears me.*

"If you take one step out of this locker room, I'm never speaking to you again."

Jaleen froze at the sound of Danni's voice. She wasn't talking loudly, but it was loud enough for him to hear on the other side of the curtain. She peeked her head through the opening.

"Did you hear what I said?"

"Um." Jaleen scratched the back of his head. "How did you know I was in here?"

"After leaving me naked on the massage table, I was hoping you'd sneak in here. I noticed you in that darkened corner when I entered."

"Damn, that makes me sound creepy."

"Not when I knew why you were in here." She opened the curtain a little more, revealing the swells of her soapy breasts. "Still want to leave?"

He glanced at her chest before meeting her eyes. "There's only one thing that will happen if I come into that shower."

She gave him a sly smile. "It better happen. Otherwise,

we wouldn't be fulfilling another item on my list." She let the curtain drop closed.

I should have known she'd guess why I was in here.

As soon as he'd learned she'd wanted to have sex in a public place, he'd known this was the perfect opportunity. He couldn't keep her waiting any longer. His body was already craving her in a way that had to be unhealthy. He removed his shorts and stepped into the shower.

Her back was to him, giving him the opportunity to observe her more closely. Her hair was pinned to the top of her head in a way he hadn't seen before, but that's not what took his breath away. The suds from her shower gel were dripping down her body, landing in creases he was itching to explore more of. It wasn't enough to stand there and watch her. He wanted to be an active participant.

He kissed the tops of her shoulders and was rewarded by another sweet moan similar to the ones he'd been hearing during her massage. Grabbing the loofah out of her hand, he began running it over her breasts, then dipped the loofah between her legs.

"We don't have much time," he whispered in her ear. "Someone could come in at any moment."

Instead of responding to him verbally, she arched her back into him and began rubbing her butt against his hardness, causing him to grow more by the second. Without warning, she turned to face him.

She nipped at his ear. "I'm not really in the mood for waiting."

Her words surged through him like a strong force that couldn't be ignored. Jaleen reached into the pocket of his shorts that he'd also draped over the side of the stall and protected them both. His lips were on hers a minute later. They hadn't kissed the entire night, so Jaleen felt like their sexual tension was at an all-time high.

Danni lifted her legs at the same time Jaleen edged them into a corner of the stall, careful to avoid getting her hair wet. He broke their kiss and held her gaze, a part of him in disbelief that he was moments away from being with the woman he thought about more than he cared to admit.

With her legs wrapped around his waist, he entered her in one long, *slow* stroke. They both moaned in satisfaction at just how right he felt buried inside her.

"I knew you'd feel amazing," he whispered to her.

"It feels so good," she said as she began to roll her hips.

Jaleen took over from there, dipping in and out of her core, each stroke better than the one before. They moved in unison as the water prickled down his back and slid over their bodies like a warm blanket. Suddenly they heard faint voices a couple of stalls down before they heard two showers turn on.

"Do you think they know we're in here together?" Danni whispered, her eyes wide in surprise.

"Maybe," Jaleen said as he continued his rhythm inside her. "But isn't that what you wanted? The possibility of getting caught?"

The fire returned to her eyes the second the words left his mouth. Her hips rejoined the pleasure, demanding as much from him as he demanded from her.

Jaleen lifted her hands above her head and clasped them in his. He'd known they hadn't had long before someone entered the locker room, but now he wished they were in the privacy of her home or his because the naughty things he wanted to do to her couldn't be done in a small stall with two other companions nearby.

Jaleen unclasped their hands so that he could reach one of his hands in between their bodies and move the other around her waist to hold her more securely. When his thumb found her sensitive nub, he twirled his thumb in lazy circles, heightening her desire.

Her catlike groan was immediate and caused him to cover her mouth with his other hand. The movement only made him want to elicit more sounds from deep within her core, so he added extra pressure to her nub and increased his movements. Moments later, Danni's entire body convulsed in a powerful orgasm that sent him soaring over the edge right with her. He must have let out an animallike groan because she placed one of her hands over his mouth while his hand remained on hers.

Jaleen eased her to the floor, allowing her body to slide down his in the process.

"We should continue this someplace else," he suggested after they'd dried and gotten dressed.

"Agreed. Should I go out first?"

"Yes. That way I can stay here until you give me the okay." Danni did exactly as they'd discussed and went back to get him when the coast was clear. She grabbed her personal belongings out of the locker just before they sneaked into the hallway.

"We were like ninjas," she said with a laugh once the door was securely shut behind them. "That was close."

"Did you two enjoy yourselves?"

Both Danni and Jaleen jumped at the voice behind them. There stood Mira with a knowing look on her face.

Jaleen leaned toward Danni's ear. "Guess we're not ninjas after all."

The elevator ride to Danni's condo seemed to take forever. Strangely, she felt nervous about taking Jaleen to her place, which made absolutely no sense. He'd been to her place before. He'd already seen her naked. They'd already had sex. True, it had been public, random, quickie sex, but that's what made it so memorable. The entire date had been amazing.

The walk down the hallway luckily seemed shorter than the elevator ride. She slightly fumbled with her keys until Jaleen finally took them from her and opened the door. Neither one of them was saying much, which was fine with Danni because she didn't know what to say anyway.

"I had fun tonight," Jaleen said, breaking the silence.

"Me, too, although some of those tantric poses were damn near impossible to do."

"They were," he said with a laugh. "Especially that boat pose. Had we been able to fully execute that one, I'm sure we would have liked it."

Danni walked over to the fridge and poured herself a glass of water. "Would you like something to drink?"

"Water's fine with me." She poured Jaleen a glass, as well, and brought it to him. They sat next to one another on the sofa as they had the day before.

"I really enjoyed the letter you wrote me," Danni said after sipping her water. "And I liked that you signed it Jay."

"I'm glad you liked it. Jay was sort of my nickname growing up. At least, to those close to me."

"Why only sort of?"

Jaleen looked into his glass of water before facing her. "Everyone calls my dad JW and I guess one day he thought that me being called Jay was too close to his name."

"Why would that even be an issue?"

"Because with JW everything is an issue."

He keeps referring to his dad as JW. She'd noticed it a couple times. Danni had already sensed that Jaleen had a strained relationship with his father, so this only solidified it. "I miss my dad every day."

"Oh, I'm sorry," Jaleen said, lightly touching her arm.

"Here I am complaining about JW when you're missing yours."

"It's okay," she said with a shrug. "I was lucky enough to have a father who loved me unconditionally and would do anything to make me happy. Our relationship was great. But I get the feeling your relationship with your father isn't so great."

"Understatement of the year," Jaleen said with a forced laugh. "Some days I wonder if I'll ever do enough to satisfy that man. He's hard on my other two brothers, as well, but especially me."

"Is he getting on your case about the South Beach renovations, too?"

"That, among other things. He agreed to an impossible deadline and although I tried to get the date pushed back, it was already a done deal by the time I returned from Europe." He put his glass down and placed his elbows on his knees. "I don't mean to sound arrogant, but out of all the men in my family who work for the company, I feel like I'm the only one who understands the vision for the future. The only one focusing on everything we're doing wrong in an effort to do more things right. I feel like my brothers and uncle are just putting out fires day by day, oblivious to the fact that JW no longer understands what's best for this company. But being the youngest means that they rarely listen to me. I don't just work at Walker Realty Partner because it's my family's business. I work my ass off because I believe in the business and I love what I do… At least, I used to love what I do."

After spending so much time with Jaleen lately, she was starting to see just how passionate he was about every aspect of his life. He was already sexy, but seeing this other side of him made him even more attractive.

Danni rubbed the back of his neck, kneading out some

kinks that had arisen. "Jay, you can only do as much as you can. I don't know your father, nor will I pretend to understand the real-estate business. But I do know that you are one of the most determined men I've ever met and if there is anyone who can make your father or your brothers and uncle see reason, it's you."

He looked at her then, searching her eyes as if they held the answers to his problems. And, boy, did she wish they did. She wanted to give him answers or, at least, offer the support he needed to solve them on his own.

She placed her glass on the table next to his and straddled his thighs. His hands looped around her waist as she placed her arms on his shoulders and fingers on the nape of his neck. "I know you feel as though you have no control over anything at your company right now, but I don't think that's going to last for long. You have to stay positive." In the back of her mind, she was trying to let her own words sink in.

When Jaleen pulled her in for a kiss, it was more emotional than any kiss he'd given her prior to that moment. He needed her. She felt it.

Danni pushed up from the couch and eased her shorts and panties down her legs, kicking them to the side. She tossed her shirt next, reaching for Jaleen's shirt and tossing it aside with her own. Jaleen stood to remove his pants and underwear before pulling out protection. When he tossed the wrapper aside, Danni slapped his hand away, enjoying the way he watched her every move as she slid the condom down his shaft.

After she'd discarded the rest of his clothes, she pushed him back on the couch. Like most of the night, words weren't needed as she slowly eased herself on top of him, relishing in every inch. Not before long, they were in perfect sync, just like before.

His head dipped to her breasts, popping one nipple into his mouth before giving the same attention to the other. She'd never really felt like she had sensitive breasts, but the way he was licking her in pleasurable strokes had her second-guessing everything she'd ever thought she enjoyed. Danni ran her hands up and down his abs, enjoying herself entirely too much to count how many he actually had.

Six? Eight? It didn't matter. It was more than the last person she was with. Hell, he was in better shape than anyone she'd ever been with. If she wasn't careful, she could get lost in a man like Jaleen. And as he picked her up and carried her to her bedroom, still buried inside her core, she feared it was already too late.

Chapter 12

Jaleen opened his sleepy eyes and glanced out the unfamiliar window at the sun rising. *Oh, that's right. I slept at Danni's place last night.* Although it was still around the same time he normally woke up, nothing about his experience last night was normal. The night had been sensual. Passionate. Downright unforgettable. There was no part of the date that he would have changed.

He reached over to the other side of the bed and found it empty. *Maybe she's in the bathroom.* He wasn't sure if she felt sore in any places, but he was hoping for another round before he went to work.

Jaleen got out of bed, and made his way to the kitchen to get a glass of water. Danni standing near the window in a sheer peach robe made him pause.

Her hair was that of a woman who'd been thoroughly made love to the night before. Her feet were bare and her body still seemed relaxed and rejuvenated. He would have sworn she'd woken up feeling just as great as he had, if her shoulders hadn't been so tense. That's when he noticed she was on the phone.

"Look, I just sent you the money yesterday and now you have the nerve to ask me for more?" She was talking low, but there was no mistaking her annoyed tone.

"I never agreed on that percentage of interest and the fact that you would try to weasel more money out of me is insane."

Who is she talking to? Could it be an ex? Jaleen doubted it was one of her brothers, although he guessed that was a possibility, as well.

"Your threats don't mean much to me anymore." *Definitely sounds more like an ex.* That's when he realized they hadn't really discussed past relationships before. He'd met a couple of guys she'd dated in the past, but none had been really serious. She'd met a few women he'd dated, but those had been even less serious.

"I only owe you three more payments and then I've fulfilled my end of the deal. Until the next payment is due, I don't want to hear from you."

A noise in the background caused her to stop talking. It took a while for Jaleen to realize that it was his phone. He sneaked back to her bedroom before she noticed.

He cursed as he glanced at the caller ID.

"Is it work?" Danni asked, standing in the doorway of her bedroom.

"Yes, it is. My lead contractor hit a slight snag. They need me there ASAP."

Danni walked over to her bed. "Back to reality, I guess."

"There's no need for us to stay in reality. We can travel back to fantasyland whenever we want." He pulled her to him and feathered kisses along her neck. "Let me know if you're free for lunch."

"Deal."

Four hours into work Jaleen realized that lunch with Danni would not be possible. Yet, just thinking about last night still made him smile.

"Is there a reason why you're grinning like a kid on the last day of school before summer break?"

Jaleen looked up from the papers in his hand at Jesse, the head of his construction team. "Can't a man just wake up and decide it's a good day to renovate some boutique hotels?"

"Yeah, some men can do that," Jesse said. "But I know you well enough to know that the look on your face isn't because you're excited to get work done today. My guess is that it's because of a woman."

Jaleen smiled. It was definitely because of a woman. A woman who'd rocked his world in a way he hadn't seen coming. Okay, maybe that wasn't completely true. He'd always imagined that being with Danni would be amazing. "What's the status on that piping issue we had this morning?"

"Ah, changing the subject. Another sign that your smile has more to do with a woman that anything else," Jesse said with a laugh. "Could it be the Southern belle waiting for you in the restaurant?"

Jaleen looked up from his documents. He hadn't gotten a chance to tell Danni he couldn't do lunch, but he'd assumed she would contact him if she could.

"I'll go see who it is," Jaleen said to Jesse. Although he was swamped, he was excited to see Danni even if it was only for a short while.

Jaleen rounded the corner of the restaurant and froze when he saw the lone feminine figure standing there with her back to him.

It can't be... Either his eyes were playing tricks on him or he'd just entered the *Twilight Zone*.

"Oh, Jaleen, darling, there you are." He could barely react before he was attacked by a hug full of ruffles. Now the fact that Jesse had referred to the woman as a Southern belle made sense.

"What are you doing here, Cordelia?" he asked, slightly more sternly than he'd been going for.

"What do you mean what am I doing here? Aren't you happy to see me?"

Happy wasn't exactly the word he would have picked. In fact, there were plenty of words that came to his mind that meant the complete opposite of the word *happy.* Cordelia Sugar Rose. In the flesh. Today, she was wearing her typical attire: a pink, ruffled dress with a large, matching straw hat. A thoroughbred Texas Southern belle, through and through.

"I'm just so happy to see you," she said, kissing his cheek. "Of course, I'd hoped you'd be a little happier to see me."

"Sorry," he said, knowing he was being rude. He put on a smile. "It's very nice to see you. I'm just surprised, that's all."

"Oh, didn't you hear?" Cordelia said, placing a hand over her heart. "I'll be here for at least two weeks appraising your South Beach properties."

His smile dropped from his face. "You're the appraiser my father told me he was sending?"

"Surprise," Cordelia said, waving her arms in the air. "JW thought it would be best if I came earlier to help speed things along."

Yeah, I highly doubt that's what he had in mind.

"Why didn't you warn me ahead of time that you would be here?"

"What's the fun in that, silly willy?" She jabbed a finger playfully into his chest. "Oh, nice." Her playful jab turned into a light caress of his chest before she was squeezing his biceps. When she batted her eyes at him, he wasn't sure if it was supposed to be sexy or if she had something in her eye.

"Can you excuse me for one moment?" he said, clawing her hands off him. "I just have to make a quick phone call."

"Well, you hurry back, honey buns."

Honey buns? If Cordelia really was staying for two weeks, he was in serious trouble. He stepped outside to call his brother.

Jeremiah answered on the first ring. "I was expecting your call around this time."

"Oh, really?" He walked farther down the block, away from the construction site. "Could it be because Cordelia just walked into one of my properties and told me she would be in South Beach for two weeks?"

"I know. JW told Joel and me this morning."

"And neither of you felt a need to tell me before she got here?"

"I did call you," Jeremiah said. "Twice. And you didn't answer."

Jaleen rubbed his forehead. "I was a little preoccupied this morning, but you could have left a voice mail or texted me."

"Look, when you were here in Chicago, JW said he'd be sending an appraiser."

"One, he never said it was Cordelia. Two, I should have had at least another week and a half before she showed up…" His voice trailed off when he heard someone yelling his name down the street. He turned to see Cordelia tripping over her heels as she tried to avoid the dips and holes on the property under construction. Jaleen dipped behind another building out of Cordelia's view.

"Bro, has she ever even worked on a construction site? She hasn't even been an appraiser for too long. This job is way too big for her and she's not experienced enough for it."

"I feel you, but you know exactly why JW sent her to South Beach."

"Of course I know why. Her being here is a smart business move and will put JW in good standing with her father. But that doesn't make it any better. That woman is a walking disaster waiting to happen."

"She's not that bad," Jeremiah said with a laugh. "Plus, she's easy on the eyes, so it will give you something pretty to look at."

"Man, how can you tell under all that mascara and big straw hat?"

After Jeremiah's laughter died down, his tone turned serious. "Listen, you know I understand what you're going through and I wish I had the words to make it easier. But the sooner you accept that JW is always going to do things his way, the sooner things will start to fall into place."

Jaleen was shaking his head even though Jeremiah couldn't see him. "You and I both know that things are only going to get worse. Joel and Uncle Jake may have their heads in the clouds, but I know you, man. You see things just like I do. The only difference is, you like to follow the rules and I like to break them. There are so many people who are afraid to stand up to JW, but his family are the only ones who know his true weakness... Failure."

Jeremiah sighed. "I know, man. I know. Listen, maybe you and I should..."

"Yoo-hoo, honey buns?"

Jaleen tensed at the sound of Cordelia's high-pitched voice.

"Did she just call you honey buns?" Jeremiah asked.

"Shut up."

"She did, didn't she?" Jeremiah's laughter barreled

through the phone. Even though Jaleen was the subject of his laughter, it was nice to hear his brother sound so carefree.

"Oh, there you are," Cordelia said from behind him. "I found you."

Did she really just change her voice to a baby tone? If there was anything Jaleen disliked more than a grade-A clinger, it was a woman who spoke to him in a baby voice. Looking at Cordelia, he wondered if she was both of his fears wrapped in one.

"Are you still on the phone?" she asked. He pointed to the phone at his ear, grateful she couldn't hear how Jeremiah was still laughing.

"When you get off, can you be a dear and carry me back to the renovation site? I can't walk through that construction again in these heels."

Carry her back? Is she serious? "Cordelia, I'm not carrying you back."

"Fine," she said, crossing her arms over her chest. "Then can you have a glass of water waiting for me since it's going to take me forever to walk back on my own."

Someone shoot me. Now. "Sure, I can do that."

"Aw, such a sweetie." With that, she turned and slowly stumbled back to the boutique hotel.

"Is she gone?" Jeremiah asked.

"Yeah, for now." Jaleen ran his fingers down his face in frustration. "I don't know how I'm going to explain her to Danni. I mean, I guess she's my appraiser, so I don't have to explain too much."

"Who's Danni?" Jeremiah asked.

Crap, did I mention her out loud?

"Wait, you're not talking about the Danni that lives in Chicago, right? The one I met at that charity auction one time. The one you just had to sit next to just to argue with her the entire night?"

"Yes, that's her."

"Damn it, Jaleen, I thought you told me you both were just friends."

"We are. I mean, we were. Now we're sort of dating." The line grew quiet. "It's pretty recent, so don't think it's been going on for years and I just haven't said anything."

"Jay, have you told her about your situation?"

"Um, not exactly."

"What does that mean?"

"It means no. I haven't told her about my situation. I've told her a little about our family and the obligations that we have to always put business first, but that's all. We're in a good place right now and I'd rather explain everything to her when the time is right."

"The time is never going to be right, little brother. If you really care about Danni, think about how hurt she will be if she finds out too late. Or worse, if you both fall for each other just to have to end your relationship at the peak of what should be the most enjoyable time for a new couple."

Jaleen grew silent as he let Jeremiah's words wash over him. He may not like what his brother was saying, but he was right. Just like Taheim had been right.

He needed to talk to Danni.

"Shit, you've already fallen for her…haven't you?" Once again, Jaleen remained quiet. "Okay, maybe you should start from the beginning."

"Come on, Danni, you're dragging," Summer said, pulling Danni along.

"I can't believe I let you talk me into bringing Jaleen lunch."

"Well, we had to meet that vendor who wants us to carry

her massage oils in the store anyway, and one of the hotels Jaleen is working on is nearby, so maybe he's here."

That's exactly what she was afraid of. She'd just had some of the best sex of her life, and now she was popping up at his job? *Can you spell* C-R-A-Z-Y?

When they arrived at the hotel, one of the construction workers said that Jaleen had stepped out.

"Oh, darn," Danni said, pretending to be disappointed. "Guess we'll just have to take these sandwiches back to the office." Danni turned to leave and bumped right into a pile of ruffled material, knocking it to the ground. No, wait. It wasn't a pile of ruffled material. It was a woman.

"I'm sorry," Danni said, trying to help the woman up but unable to find her arms.

"Isn't this just a soupy bag of grits," the woman said in a deep Southern accent. "Can you be a doll and help me up?"

"I'm trying," Danni said, nodding to Summer so she could help, too. Together they got her to her feet.

"There, that's better." The woman adjusted her oversize hat and smoothed out her dress as much as Danni assumed it could be smoothed given all the ruffles.

"I'm Cordelia Sugar Rose," she said, extending her hand. "My mom gave me that middle name because I came out the womb tasting as sweet as pie every time she kissed me."

"Is this chick serious?" Summer whispered to Danni.

"And you two are?" Cordelia asked.

Summer nudged for her to go first.

"Um, I'm Danni Allison." Danni accepted her handshake.

"Summer Dupree-Chase," Summer said, doing the same. "Nice to meet you."

"I heard you were here to see Jaleen Walker. May I ask why?"

"We're friends of his," Summer said. "And you are?"

"Well, I'm an old friend of Le Le's." Cordelia brushed some of her hair out of her face, which caused her to slightly lose her balance.

Danni could see a pretty girl peeking from underneath all that fluff, but she had on so much material she might as well be wearing a costume.

"Is Le Le expecting you?" Cordelia queried sweetly.

Le Le? She's called him that twice. Danni glanced at Summer in time to see her try to stifle a laugh.

"Can I ask why you call him Le Le?" Danni asked. Cordelia didn't strike her as Jaleen's type of old friend.

"Well, yes, you see, I'm—"

"She's my appraiser," Jaleen said, walking through the door. "I didn't know you ladies were stopping by."

Danni didn't miss the look of annoyance he sent Cordelia's way.

"We were in the area, so we figured we'd bring you lunch," Summer said.

"We brought you a sandwich." Danni handed him the bag, her hand brushing his as she did so. Memories from last night came rushing to the forefront of her mind. Judging by the way he looked as if he wanted to drag her to the nearest corner and make love to her all over again, she assumed he was having the same thoughts.

Someone loudly clearing their throat got her attention. They both turned to face Cordelia who was giving Danni a not-so-friendly stare.

"Cordelia, don't you have to check out another property right now?" Jaleen asked.

"Yes, I suppose I do," she said, straightening her back and walking out the room. Only then did Summer release her laugh.

"Seriously, Jaleen, did you, like, date her and she never got over it or something?" Summer asked. "Is she really a childhood friend?" Danni smiled at Summer. She may have disguised her question as a joke, but girlfriend had her back.

"No, we never dated. She's from Texas and, yes, I guess you can say we've been friends since we were kids. She's not all that bad. Just different."

And really has a crush on you. Danni wasn't even the type to get jealous, so there was no use starting now. "We really should be getting back to the shop," she said, nodding at Summer.

"Oh, right. 'Bye, Jaleen."

Danni looked up at him before leaving. "See you later."

"Wait, that's it?" Jaleen asked, touching her on the arm.

"What do you mean?"

He didn't make her wait long to understand his meaning. When he pulled her into a passionate kiss, she instantly melted against his body.

"Okay," he said, giving her one more peck. "Now I'm good."

As Danni walked out the door, she felt like she was in a daze. A really dreamy daze as a result of a great kiss.

"Aren't you glad we brought him that sandwich?" Summer asked.

Yes, she was glad she'd brought him that sandwich. Unfortunately now she wished she'd given him a lot more than that.

Chapter 13

"Danni, are you okay?"

Danni turned to face Summer, who was standing with Nicole and Aaliyah.

"Yes, I'm fine. Just trying to finalize a few things before we head to Chicago."

Danni, Summer and Aiden were headed to Chicago for sweet baby Emma's first birthday party. Winter and Taheim were beyond ecstatic and Danni had no doubt that the couple had planned an extravagant birthday for their baby girl.

At first, Danni had considered skipping the trip when Jaleen informed her that he wouldn't be able to go. Then she'd remembered that Winter would kill her if she missed her child's first birthday. It was more than a gathering for the young one. It was a way for everyone to see each other now that folks were living in different states and even different countries.

"I know what it is." Nicole's voice broke through her thoughts. "You're disappointed that Jaleen won't be there."

"No, I'm not," Danni said quickly. "I'm just making a mental to-do list of everything I have to do when I get back from Chicago." That was only partially true. She hadn't seen Jaleen since she'd taken him lunch a week ago. Although he'd called and texted her a few times, she got the distinct feeling that something else was going on. Something she couldn't quite place her finger on. She was hoping they would have gotten a chance to discuss things in Chicago, but he'd texted her a couple of days ago to let her know that he couldn't go.

"Is everything okay with you two?" Summer asked. "Because I have no problem cursing him out if he's treating you badly. I've seen that man in action before, so I know how he can be."

"No, that's not it. You know I've seen him in action, too, but he doesn't treat me like he treats other women. But I still get the sense that something is wrong. Up until last week, it seemed he would go out of his way to see me. Now it almost seems as if he's making up excuses as to why he can't."

"You still have two more dates left, right?" Aaliyah asked. "I can't imagine Jaleen passing up the opportunity to collect on his last two dates."

"Danni, you seem mentally exhausted and if Jaleen is the cause, then I think I'll stick with my instinct and curse him out anyway," Summer added.

She was sure she looked exhausted because she definitely felt exhausted. However, she didn't have bags under her eyes because of Jaleen. It was because of the series of threatening phone calls she'd received every day for the past week. The first call came the morning after her third date with Jaleen. She'd refused to let the caller bait her into giving more money than the agreed-upon amount. When the call had ended, Danni had assumed she'd gotten her point across, until the phone calls started coming back-to-back from different numbers. It was so bad that she was contemplating getting another phone number.

"I can handle it," she said to Summer. "I have a lot more going on than just my issues with Jaleen."

"Anything we can help with?" Nicole asked.

Danni looked at each woman, appreciating their friendship but knowing she wasn't ready to discuss anything with them. Besides, she'd have to have a few private conversations before that time came anyway.

"How about this?" Danni said. "If I think of a way for either of you to help, I promise to let you know."

They seemed satisfied with the answer. Aiden came through the door a few moments later to pick up her and Summer. That was another thing she loved about having friends like Nicole and Aaliyah who were so dedicated to the store. Whenever she or Summer had to go to Chicago, the store was always left in good hands.

The plane ride to Chicago was smooth sailing. Not only were there no delays, but they made it with hours to spare before the birthday party. Just as Danni had expected, Winter and Taheim had gone all out for Emma's birthday. Taheim's parents' backyard was fully decked out with inflatables, a candy station, enough food to feed an army, a gorgeous princess cake and even a petting zoo area with a few animals.

As the night died down, the children had all gone and the only people that were left were the adults. Taheim's parents took baby Emma after lighting their huge bonfire. Although there were still adults sprinkled throughout the backyard, Danni was sitting in a circle with Winter, Autumn and Summer, as well as their husbands. *Why do I feel so awkward?* She'd been around this particular group of couples for a while and she'd never felt out of place before. Like a seventh wheel. She might as well be wearing a big neon sign that said Lonely Seat for One.

That's because Jaleen's usually here.

They'd never been a couple, but he was always usually around since he was Taheim's best friend. Even when she hadn't wanted him to be, Jaleen would show up anyway. In a way, Danni had been Jaleen's wingwoman just as much as he'd been her wingman. Despite the fact that they used to never get along, the group sitting around the fire had always paired them together. She supposed that's why it felt so strange not having him there. They shared so many friends that he'd been a constant person in her life over the past few years.

"Did you enjoy the party?" Winter asked, leaning closer to her.

"Yes," Danni said, shaking away her thoughts. "It was beautiful and Emma was so happy the entire day."

"That's our little princess," Winter said with a smile. "She knew the day was about her, so she acted the part."

"She did," Danni said with a laugh. "I'm glad I came."

"Even though Jaleen couldn't make it?"

"Why does everyone keep asking me that? Jaleen being or not being at an event doesn't define my happiness. He's not here and I'm having a good time. If he were here, I'd still be having a good time. It doesn't matter."

Winter gave her a look of disbelief. "Who are you trying to convince? Me or you?"

Danni looked away and gazed into the fire. Who was she trying to convince? "I don't even know," she answered honestly.

"Don't know what?" Summer asked as she and Autumn sat with her and Winter.

"She doesn't know if she wishes Jaleen were here or if she's glad he isn't."

"Oh, that." Summer waved her hand in the air. "We just

went through this before our flight today. I'm not sure we concluded on an answer."

Autumn observed her a little closer. "Judging by the starry-eyed gaze she's been in most of the night, I'd say she wishes he were here."

"You guys are hilarious," Danni said with a laugh. "Remind me never to get involved in your love life again."

"It's too late for that," Summer said. "You were all up in my love life when I was trying to figure out my feelings for Aiden."

Winter nodded her head in agreement. "You were in mine, too, when it came to Taheim."

Danni glanced at Autumn, expecting her to say something next.

"I'm not even going to go there," Autumn said. "Because you were telling all my business to my sisters. I partially blame you for being the reason Ajay and I had to elope."

"That wasn't my fault," Danni said. "We all know that although you believe in love and marriage, you aren't too fond of weddings."

"That's true," Autumn said with a laugh. "We originally thought we could handle all the frill and fuss. But Ajay and I were so involved with Winter and Taheim's wedding, it seemed only fitting that we elope after Summer told us she was engaged to Aiden."

Winter rolled her eyes. "I still can't believe you eloped. Especially after wedding plans were already under way. You're lucky Summer got engaged and I was able to channel my energy into her wedding because otherwise, I would have disowned you and my brother-in-law."

Autumn smiled at Winter. "Our quickie wedding was perfect and Ajay and I loved the overpriced reception you and Taheim threw for us after we returned."

All the women shared a laugh. Out of all the couples,

Danni found the most joy in teasing Autumn about Ajay. "Autumn, you were hands-down the most interesting love story to watch unfold."

"Hey," Summer said, hitting Danni on the shoulder. "I'm your favorite, so I should have been the best story, Sherlock Danni."

Winter and Autumn rolled their eyes, as they often did when Summer got territorial over Danni. Technically, Danni had known Winter and Autumn for longer than she'd known Summer. But the two had immediately connected and formed a strong bond.

Danni glanced at each of the women who'd become much more than just friends to her over the years. She honestly couldn't imagine the last three years without them. Each woman was unique in her own way and although they were the Dupree sisters, they were different in so many ways.

I've always wanted that bond with siblings. While she had an older and younger brother, she'd always missed the closeness that came with having a sister. *That's probably why I'm so close to my mom.* She guessed that some couldn't have the best of both worlds because the Dupree sisters had the worst mom on the planet, whereas Danni would give her right arm to her mom if she needed it.

But you've made some bad decisions lately. Decisions that hurt your mom...

The thought crept into her mind quicker than she could block it. Her mom was the only person on earth who knew about the poor decisions she'd made, and yet she loved her unconditionally anyway. Her mother had a beautiful spirit and Danni was blessed to have her in her life.

Danni felt her heartbeat quicken and her hands grow clammy, a sign that a panic attack was brewing. *Oh, no, not now.* Lately she'd been getting them more and more, the triggers harder to recognize now than they had been before.

She noticed the look of concern on Autumn's face first, but she couldn't hear what she was saying. Her mind was blocked. Before she knew it, all three women were shoving water bottles in her face and waving their arms in what she assumed was their way of trying to get her to focus. She wanted to tell them it was of no use. That everything they were saying was just background noise to the buzzing she heard in her head.

It's probably my own fault. Since she was the one who had made poor decisions, then it was her fault that she was having sudden panic attacks. This one was worse than usual, especially with all her friends there to witness it and panic right along with her since they didn't know what to do.

Now the men were involved, which was making it even worse because there were too many bodies to focus on, making it harder for her to concentrate on just one person.

"Back up everyone, you're too close to her." *Jaleen?* She knew that voice. Knew that scent.

"Danni, it's me." *It is him.* "Focus on your breathing. Like we did in yoga class."

But what is he doing here? She half thought she was imagining his voice, until he came clearly into view, fading out the other faces of concern surrounding him. She listened to his words.

"That's it, baby. Just like the instructor taught us."

That is definitely his voice. And she'd never been more relieved to hear a voice in her life. When all the buzzing and white noise cleared, all she saw was him. All she heard was him.

"Welcome back, beautiful," Jaleen said, lightly rubbing her cheeks. "I think you've officially scared all our friends."

Danni glanced around the group, which did indeed look as if she'd given them each a panic attack, as well.

"I must have looked like a nutcase," she said low so only he could here.

"A beautiful, sexy nutcase." He kissed the tip of her nose. "You've been getting panic attacks a lot, haven't you?"

She searched his eyes. "How did you know?"

"Because I get the feeling we still have a lot to talk about." He pressed his forehead to hers. "And I've experienced a few of my own."

Instead of going to her hotel, Danni took Jaleen up on his offer to stay at his penthouse. He was glad she'd accepted his offer because if she hadn't, he probably would have asked if he could stay with her instead. It hadn't taken long to grab her belongings and check out of the hotel.

When he'd entered the Reeds' backyard and seen everyone crowded around Danni, he'd thought his heart had literally stopped. However, when he'd reached her and was able to assess the situation, he knew exactly what was happening and had acted quickly.

"You didn't tell me you were coming," Danni said as she kicked off her shoes.

"I was trying my best to see if I could get away from work for a quick trip, but I wasn't sure. The South Beach properties have been giving me hell. I hate that I still missed almost the entire party, but I'm glad I got there when I did."

Danni smiled. "Me, too."

You flew across several states to see that smile.

"Do you mind if I take a quick shower? Between the

petting zoo, helping a few of the kids build ice cream sundaes and holding baby Emma while she threw up after Aiden spun her one too many times, I think it's necessary."

Jaleen quirked an eyebrow. "A petting zoo?"

"Oh, yeah," she said with a laugh. "Equipped with an actual pony."

"Crap, I missed the pony rides."

Danni was laughing so hard, he could still hear her after she'd shut the bathroom door. Truthfully, Jaleen had wanted to see Danni, too, because he wasn't sure he could go another day without clearing the air. He cared about her too much not to tell her what was going on. Whenever he thought about his situation, he just got angry.

Tonight, I'll tell her everything. Even reinforcing the plans he'd spent his entire plane ride thinking about did little to ease his tension. The last thing he wanted was to lose her completely. That couldn't happen. He wouldn't let it.

She'd be out of the shower any minute now and when she came out, he had to ease into the conversation as he'd practiced.

Jaleen stood to pour two glasses of the wine he'd picked up after landing, when something caught his eye.

He glanced at the folded sheet of paper sticking out of her open suitcase. *That's got to be her list.* The creases in the paper were worn, as if it had been opened and refolded numerous times before. He'd been curious about the last couple items on it ever since she'd mentioned they were items she wouldn't share with him because she kept them too close to her heart.

Although he was anxious to know what those extremely personal items were, he refused to betray her trust by reading her list without her permission. Given how much their relationship had matured over the past few weeks, he hoped she would eventually feel comfortable enough to discuss the rest of her list. If not, he'd have to settle for not knowing.

"Were you debating on reading my list?" she asked, coming out the bathroom wrapped in only a towel. She'd washed her hair so her natural curls were clipped atop her head in a messy bun that made him want to discard the clip and busy his fingers within. Her natural Danni glow combined with the way her skin glistened from her shower was beyond sexy. His eyes left her face, stopping briefly at her mouth before trailing down to her legs. He wanted to take her again. Right there.

"Um, no. I noticed it was your list, but I promised you I wouldn't look at it without your permission and I plan on keeping my promise."

A look of disappointment crossed her face, but that didn't make any sense. She was the one who'd made him promise. "That's the promise you asked me to make, right?"

"Yes, you're right," she said, making her way to the bed. "I was just wondering if maybe I should discuss that last item with you…but I'm nervous."

He studied her face, trying to see if she was being serious. *She is… She needs to talk to someone.* He understood how she would feel that way after her panic attack. Hell, it was probably the same reason he wanted to talk to her.

"Maybe this will help." He handed her a glass of wine, then sat in a nearby chair while Danni sat on the bed.

"Thanks," she said, taking a sip before placing it on the table. "Let me just put on some clothes."

As he watched her walk away, he wanted to tell her that clothes were overrated. But she already seemed nervous to discuss whatever was on her list. He'd let her discuss what she needed to tell him and then he'd tell her what he should have told her months before.

Chapter 14

"Okay, Danni. You can do this," she chanted to the bathroom mirror for a third time, trying to boost her confidence. A few hours ago she wasn't even sure what was going on with Jaleen. She hadn't seen him in a week and although she hadn't said it aloud, she'd feared he was already thinking things were moving too fast. And, who knows, he could still be feeling that way.

But she couldn't worry about that right now because, after the last panic attack, she knew her problem had escalated to an all-time high. She needed to talk to someone. Her mom only knew half the story and, quite frankly, she didn't want her mom to worry about her any more than she already did.

Jaleen was someone she could lean on for support and advice, but only if he didn't push her away after he learned the truth. "Am I really about to do this?" she asked herself. After years of keeping the information to herself, was she really about to reveal the truth to Jaleen? A man who, up until a year ago, was holding down the number-one spot on her "People I Often Want to Strangle" list? Well, maybe not the number-one spot, but he was definitely in the top three.

She studied her reflection once more before exiting the

bathroom. She found Jaleen still sitting in the chair with what she assumed was his second glass of wine. She retrieved her glass and sat on the bed, facing him directly. She glanced at the folded sheet of paper that was in her suitcase as she took a sip of wine.

"Do you want your list?" he asked.

She shook her head. "Don't need it." They sat in silence for what felt like an hour, which in reality had only been about five minutes. He was patiently waiting for her to talk, but she didn't feel anywhere near ready to.

Jaleen put down his glass and moved the chair closer toward her. He touched her thighs, rubbing his thumb in soothing circles before his hands settled on her knees. "Is there anything I can do to make this easier for you?"

God, I must look like such a baby. She was a grown woman holding on to her secret as if saying it out loud would be the end of the world. But she supposed in some ways, it would. There are a lot of people who would be hurt if she delivered the news in the wrong way, including the man sitting across from her.

"I still don't want you to see my entire list... So what if I write down number thirty since I've memorized it?"

"Okay," Jaleen said. "Whatever you want to do is fine with me. Danni, I've done a lot of things, seen a lot of things. It's probably not as bad a secret as you think. I'm not saying that your nervousness isn't warranted, but I know the type of woman you are, so whatever it is, I'll support you."

She instantly closed her eyes to block out the tears she felt would creep in any minute. "You're speaking prematurely... You may think you know me, but maybe you should wait to make promises until you know what it is."

She grabbed her notepad out of her suitcase instead. Even as she began writing, her hands were shaking. She only had to write five words. Five words. Yet the meaning behind them was life changing.

Slowly she handed Jaleen the notepad.

"Should I read it out loud?"

She nodded her head.

"Okay, it says…'tell my sisters the truth.'"

He looked up at her, confusion evident on his face. "I didn't know you had sisters. What do you have to tell them?"

He's not going to make this easy. "I have to tell them that I'm their sister." She fidgeted with the pen in her hand and looked at him expectantly.

"You don't know them?"

"I do now." *Go ahead, Danni! Tell him!* "Years ago, they didn't have a name." She noticed the moment he began to piece it together. "But now, I know them as Winter, Autumn and Summer."

Jaleen's hand flew to his face as his mouth dropped. She'd never seen his eyes that big before. "Oh, shit," he finally said.

"I know." She searched his eyes for any emotion other than shock. "*Shit* would be an accurate word."

"You're their sister."

"Yes."

"Blood sister."

She squinted in confusion. "Yes, we share a parent." He still looked shocked, which was doing little to ease her discomfort.

"You have the same father?"

Danni glanced out the bedroom window before looking back at Jaleen. "No, we share the same mother."

"That god-awful woman I've been hearing about for years is your mother?" Anger replaced the shock in his eyes so quickly she didn't have time to react.

The tears began to well in Danni's eyes. *I'd never call that horrible woman "mother."*

"She may not have given birth to me, but Regina Allison is my mom in all the ways that matter."

Jaleen rose from the chair and sat right next to her on the bed, pulling her into his embrace. As her tears began to fall, she felt him pull her in even tighter, offering her comfort that she desperately needed.

"She's the reason you're having panic attacks, isn't she?"

Danni lifted her tear-streaked face to Jaleen. "What makes you say that?"

He wiped a few of her tears away. "Because even though I had no idea that you were sisters with Winter, Autumn and Summer, I can smell blackmail a mile away. Last week, when I spent the night at your place, I heard the end of your phone conversation. Was she the person you were speaking to?"

She hadn't planned on telling him this much tonight and she definitely didn't want to discuss Sonia Dupree. But he'd asked and she wanted to give him an honest answer. She'd spent too many years trying to cover up lies, so it was time she started telling the truth.

"Yes, Sonia was the person I was talking to." Danni sighed deeply. "She's still trying to blackmail me and for almost two years, she's been doing a damn good job at it. The call you heard was me telling her that I was done being blackmailed. Needless to say, the call didn't go that well and now I'm afraid I've only made matters worse."

Jaleen looked from Danni to the five words written on the paper as if they would give him clarity that he could only get from asking her more questions. *Danni is Winter, Autumn and Summer's sister?* He still couldn't believe it. When she'd been agonizing over an item on her list, he had no idea that it would have been such a huge secret.

There's no way you can tell her what you wanted to now. After the bomb she'd just dropped on him, he couldn't imagine dropping one on her in the same night.

"When did you find out that Sonia was your mother?"

Danni adjusted herself on the bed. "When my dad got sick seven years ago, he kept telling me that he had something important to discuss. But I was so worried about his health that I kept disregarding his wishes, diverting the subject any chance I got."

"You had a feeling it was something huge, didn't you?"

"Yes, I did. Even though my dad was sick, my mom and older brother had been extra attentive to me. It was almost like they knew what was coming and they were trying to let me know I had their love and support no matter what. On the day my parents told me that Regina wasn't my birth mom, he had been sick for two years. I cried, yelled, cried some more, yelled some more.

"My older brother came to me and told me that he remembered the first day he'd met me and knew in that moment I'd forever be his sister even though we didn't share the same birth parents. Unlike me, he knew my dad wasn't his birth father. The only person that knew less than me was my younger brother. After hours of feeling as if I no longer knew my place in my family, I thought about the first time I'd suspected that the mom I knew and loved wasn't actually my birth mother."

Jaleen began stroking her legs.

"When I was twelve," she continued, "I was messing around in my dad's shed. The shed he'd never wanted us to go into. I remember climbing this ladder he kept in the corner and looking frantically on his shelf for something I'd thought he'd put there when he placed me on punishment. I can't even remember what I'd been looking for anymore."

Danni brush a few curls from her face. "I remember knocking a box to the ground and stuff splattering everywhere. When I went to pick it all up, there were four pictures scattered around that I hadn't seen before. Two of the pictures were of my dad with this woman who had long, dark hair. I flipped over the back of the photo and it said 'Sonia.' That was it. They looked so happy and I remember thinking that my dad had never mentioned an ex named Sonia before. But it was the last two pictures that had given me chills. They were of Sonia pregnant. Both of her by herself. I remember looking at the pictures of her swollen belly and thinking about the fact that I'd never seen pictures of my mom pregnant with me, yet my dad had pictures of this woman? I felt close to the picture somehow, which hadn't made any sense. At twelve, I didn't understand, so I put them back exactly how I'd found them and rushed out of the shed."

"That must have been so hard to discover," Jaleen said. "Being twelve and not knowing how to decipher something important that you stumbled upon."

"It was. I'd never forgotten what I saw and in a way, I guess it happened that way for a reason. My dad met my mom Regina when I was only three months old. She was a single mother with her own babysitting business. Whoever was supposed to watch me called in sick, so she came instead. They'd never really discussed the details of how they met before, so it was nice to finally hear the true story."

"So you and Summer are extremely close in age," Jaleen said, doing a few mental calculations.

"Yes, we're actually thirteen months apart. I guess Sonia had Summer and then ran off when she was a baby. She met my dad, got pregnant with me a month later, then took off when I wasn't even three months old and went back to her family."

That woman is a piece of work. Jaleen remembered Taheim talking about Sonia Dupree after the one and only time he'd met her. Jaleen hadn't liked anything he'd heard. "Danni, what is she blackmailing you for? How did she even find you, because from what I heard, she isn't the type of mother to seek out her daughters?"

"You're right," Danni said. "She is definitely not the type to seek out her daughters, however, she is the type to exploit them. She didn't have to find me because I went looking for her after my dad passed away. I wanted to hear her side of the story. My dad didn't know her as the Sonia we hear about, so I didn't know what I was getting into before I tracked her down. She was easy to find since a quick Google search lead me to the Vegas show she was headlining. So I went there to meet her."

"Wait a second," Jaleen said, piecing even more together. "You knew she was headlining at that show before Winter and her sisters knew?"

"Yes," Danni said sheepishly. "And she is as horrible as you've heard. The meeting was so bad, I vowed to never look up anyone else with the last name Dupree."

Jaleen searched her eyes. "But, instead, you decided to give your search one more try and then you found the Dupree sisters, right?"

"Right," she said, nodding her head. "More specifically, I found the Bare Sophistication website announcing that a new boutique was coming to Chicago. I majored in business management and had worked at numerous retail and boutique stores, so when I noticed the opening for the store manager position, I figured that was my chance to meet my birth sisters."

"Only Sonia had left a bad taste in your mouth."

"Exactly. There was no way I was walking into the store and announcing who I was. I figured I could work with them for a week or two, get to know them, then tell them the truth."

Danni briefly glanced at the ceiling with a faraway look in her eyes. "I never expected them to end up being some of the best friends I've ever had. Suddenly I was making up excuses to myself as to why I couldn't tell them the truth."

Jaleen cringed, knowing all too well exactly what she meant. He was going through his own inner struggles deciding the right time to tell Danni his secrets. "I understand," he said. "More than you probably realize."

When she turned back to face him, he saw the years of struggling to tell the truth written on her face. He also saw a hint of relief that she'd been able to tell the truth to at least one person.

"How is Sonia blackmailing you?"

Danni sighed. "She found out I had gotten the job at Bare Sophistication. I assumed it was because there were a couple of PR announcements that had my name and they had me added to the website. I'd left my cell phone number and name with one of the security guards for her show when I didn't think I would get a chance to meet her. I assume she got my number from him. After I'd been working there for about three months, she called to ask if I'd said anything to Winter, Autumn and Summer. I said no and didn't hear from her until almost two years ago, when her Vegas show began struggling to produce numbers. She called and threatened to tell Winter, Autumn and Summer who I was and the only way for her to keep her silence was for me to pay her a monthly fee."

"That's ridiculous," Jaleen said, growing more annoyed the more he thought about it.

"I know. But at the time I was enjoying my time with Winter and Autumn so much that I didn't want Sonia to ruin it. And I'd just gotten a chance to get to know Summer. So I agreed to pay her."

"I understand why you did it. But a woman like that will never be satisfied. Take it from someone who has a father just like her." Jaleen supposed that's why he'd known the caller had to be Sonia after Danni had told him her true identity. He'd seen those same Sonia qualities reflected in his own father.

"You're right, she's never satisfied. I already pay her every month and now she wants payments every third week. I did some digging around and I found out they just canceled her Vegas show. She went from doing shows five days a week to three, down to two, until they finally canceled it altogether. So I assume that's why her calls have gotten more frantic."

He cracked his neck, trying to ease the knot he felt developing.

"Are you okay?" she asked in a soft voice.

Was he okay? He wasn't sure. "I don't like you being blackmailed by Sonia. There has to be something we can do."

"Jay, as much as it touches my heart that you want to help me, I'm not dragging you into my mess. You'll be happy to know that I've already stopped paying Sonia, which is why she's been harassing me or manipulating her friends into calling me. But I finally know how to solve the problem."

"How?"

"By doing exactly what I should have done in the first place," Danni said as if she had the weight of one thousand camels on her back. "Winter and Autumn asked Summer and I if we could meet about our upcoming plans to ensure the Chicago and Miami stores are aligned tomorrow. I can't wait any longer, or worse, let Sonia spill the beans. Tomorrow I finally tell Winter, Autumn and Summer the truth."

Chapter 15

"Danni, if you walk any slower, you'll be walking backward."

"I can't help it," she said as she glanced at Jaleen. "I just told you all this information last night and now, less than twenty-fours later, I'm telling Winter, Autumn and Summer. What am I thinking?"

Jaleen stopped walking and gently grabbed both of her arms. "You don't have to do this today if you don't want to. You can wait until you're ready. I know you're worried about Sonia getting to your sisters before you do, but we can try to figure out another way to hold off Sonia."

Danni smiled. "You called them my sisters."

"That's because they are and no matter how nervous you are to tell them or how afraid you are of how they will handle the news, it won't change the fact that the four of you are sisters."

She was already feeling more confident, which meant the pep talk was working.

Oh, no, the partnership. "And don't worry about the partnership. You may have withheld this information from them, but it won't take away from the fact that you would be the best partner they could ever have. You love Bare Sophistication just as much as they do."

It was true. She lived and breathed Bare Sophistication. She believed in their vision just as much as they did. "How did you know I was worried about that?"

"When will you learn, Danni Allison," Jaleen said, placing a quick kiss on her lips, "I notice everything about you. I figured there had to be a reason you were putting off the partnership for so long when it seemed like a dream come true for you."

She was still reeling about how well Jaleen knew her when they walked into Bare Sophistication. Everyone else was already there.

"Fellas," Ajay said with a whistle, "let's head down the street so you can check out one of the sports bars I just purchased."

"I'm only a text or phone call away if you need me," Jaleen whispered in her ear. "You'll do great. Just speak from the heart." Their kiss was brief, but just what she needed.

"Okay, ladies," Winter said, "let's go to my studio to get this show on the road before the store opens."

Danni had taken the walk down the hall to Winter's studio numerous times, but this was the first time she felt like she was taking the walk of doom. *How am I going to get through this?* In hindsight, the idea had seemed a lot easier to execute last night when she'd been talking to Jaleen.

"Okay, so first things first," Winter said, clasping her hands together. "How cute were Jaleen and Danni yesterday evening?"

Danni laughed. "How is that the first order of business?"

"Um, maybe because you were having a massive panic attack and none of us could calm you down," Summer said. "Then, lo and behold, Jaleen appears out of thin air and basically forces us all to back away from you so that he can take charge and, lucky you, his was the only voice you actually heard."

She thought about how Jaleen had arrived at the party at just the right time. "I have to admit, besides the fact that I was having one of the worst panic attacks I've had in weeks, having Jaleen come to my rescue and be the sole person to calm me down is a moment I won't forget anytime soon."

"Why have you been having so many panic attacks?" Autumn asked. "All jokes aside, you scared the crap out of us yesterday."

"Oh, you know…" Danni said with a shrug. "Just the normal stressful stuff."

"When did your panic attacks start?" Autumn frowned in observation. "The other day, I read that about six million Americans over the age of eighteen suffer from panic attacks and about three percent of that group has an actual panic disorder."

"Autumn, I can assure you that I do not have a panic disorder."

Autumn looked unconvinced. "I'll do some research on the percentage of those with the disorder that go undiagnosed."

"Okay, Queen of Stats," Summer said, rolling her eyes, "can we go back to the part about Danni saying that the moment she had with Jaleen was one she'd never forget before you realize she has any other disorders?"

As the women laughed, Danni looked from one to the other, wishing she could bottle up this moment just like she would the one with Jaleen.

"On a more serious note…" Summer said, looking solely at Danni. "I've even noticed at the store that you've been under a lot of stress. This isn't the first time I've seen you have a panic attack, but this was by far the worst I've seen. I don't know why, but I have this feeling in my gut that something is wrong with you and I can't quite place what it is."

Summer glanced at Autumn and Winter before looking back at Danni. "We've also realized that, for some reason, you haven't signed the paperwork needed to solidify our partnership. Our feelings won't be hurt if it's something you no longer want, but we can't help but feel like there's more to it than that."

She must have looked like a deer caught in headlights because Winter came to sit next to her and grabbed her hand. "Danni, whatever it is, you can tell us." Winter was the nurturing one. The one to go to if you needed a hug or just wanted someone to listen to you.

"We can sense that something's wrong. The hardest part is opening up." That was Autumn. The one who always had a solution to your problem. If she didn't know how to help you, she'd find someone who did.

"We've got your back," Summer said with a smile. "Always."

It was Summer that caused Danni's eyes to water. She felt close to all three women, but she'd forged a bond with Summer that she hoped couldn't be broken. She didn't know if it was because they were so close in age or because they shared so many of the same interests and now saw each other almost every day. Summer was the one Danni knew she could call to not talk her out of a fight but to fight right beside her. They were all one of a kind and it broke her heart that what she had to tell them meant she may lose them forever.

Danni's heart was pounding so hard, she worried that the ladies could see it beating out of her chest. *I think this is it. This is the perfect time.* In all honesty, she knew the perfect time had come and gone for her, but this was the closest to it.

"All of you are right. There has been something huge weighing heavily on my heart for a while now." She looked at each of the women. "I know you said that you'll always have my back and that I can tell you anything, but what I'm about to tell you puts me in jeopardy of losing you ladies forever."

"That could never happen," Summer said as her eyes began to water.

How many times had one started crying that in turn made the other start crying? More times than Danni could count.

"You're going to hate me for this."

"We could never hate you," Winter said.

Danni took a deep breath. "Winter and Autumn, do you remember the day I arrived here to interview for the manager position?"

"Of course," Autumn said as Winter nodded her head in agreement.

"Well, I didn't come here by accident..." She stopped talking when she heard a loud bang on the window.

"Who the heck is banging on the window like that?" Summer said as she stood from her seat. The banging continued, growing louder and more frantic.

"Let's see who it is," Winter said, with the rest of them following behind her.

"Oh, my God," Winter said when she turned the corner. "What the hell is she doing here?"

Danni vaguely heard Summer and Autumn say something to Winter, but she couldn't speak or add to the conversation. The cat literally had her tongue, or in this case, staring at Sonia Dupree in the flesh had cut off her ability to speak.

"Why do you keep looking at your phone?" Taheim asked.

"No reason."

"Really? Because it looks to me like you're expecting Danni to text or call you or something."

Jaleen glanced at Taheim. "Why do you care if I'm looking at my phone?"

"Somebody's in a foul mood today," Ajay said. "What's wrong with you, man?"

"Nothing wrong with me. I was just wondering why Taheim won't mind his own business."

Jaleen was acting like he was on edge, but he didn't care. Ever since he'd left Danni, he'd been wondering how her conversation was going with her sisters. It wasn't even his information to tell, yet he felt almost as nervous as Danni about the conversations he'd have to have after she spoke with her sisters, as well.

He smiled. *I'm talking as if we are a couple.*

They may not be married, but Jaleen had strong feelings for Danni and, in all the ways that counted, he did feel like they were a couple.

"I know what it is," Aiden said, breaking his thoughts. "You've fallen in love with Danni, haven't you?"

Taheim's eyes flew to Jaleen's. His accusatory stare left nothing to question. He hadn't talked to Danni yet and Taheim knew it. Taheim's phone vibrated, breaking the staredown between them.

"You've got to be kidding me," Taheim said, reading his text. "Sonia Dupree just showed up at the shop."

"She did?" Jaleen asked. "What did she say? What's going on?"

Ajay gave him a confused look. "Do you even know who Sonia is?"

"Of course I do," he said, looking at the guys. "It's Winter, Autumn and Summer's mom. Did Winter say any more in the text?"

The men were ignoring him. Probably because they assumed he was the only one who was unaware of the type of person Sonia was.

"We'd better get to the shop," Aiden said. "I don't need that woman insulting my wife, nor do I want any of them there alone with her."

Jaleen followed the men to the boutique, anxious to stand by Danni's side. When they arrived, Sonia was standing outside the shop and the ladies were watching her from the inside.

At first, Jaleen couldn't find Danni. Then he noticed her in the corner of the shop, hiding behind a fixture to try to remain unseen. He took one look at Danni and knew she hadn't been able to tell her sisters the truth, which meant this situation was about to get a whole lot worse.

Seeing Jaleen outside the boutique's door was bittersweet. Winter, Autumn and Summer had agreed not to let Sonia in until the men had arrived. Only then would they see what she wanted before sending her on her way.

For obvious reasons, Danni hadn't gotten a vote. Now it felt like the entire situation was a ticking time bomb waiting to explode.

"We can open the door now," Winter said. "The men are here, so I doubt she'll try anything too crazy."

I wouldn't be too sure about that.

Watching Winter unlock the door and Sonia burst through with unnecessary force was like one of those bad overdramatic shows that always liked to show scenes in slow motion.

"It's about damn time you opened up that door for me," Sonia said loudly.

Danni felt movement at her side and turned to face Jaleen. She couldn't be sure, but she didn't think Sonia had noticed she was in the room yet.

"I came bearing some really juicy news. News that I know you'll want to hear." Sonia waved her arms as if she were still doing her Vegas stage show. "But you see, I don't just give away shit for free. So if you want to know what I have to share, you better be willing to pay top dollar."

"Why would we ever give you anything?" Autumn said. "You don't mean anything to us and I'm sure that news is as useless as you are."

"My, my, Autumn. Your mouth has gotten a lot fouler than I remember. Trust me, you'll want to know this information." Sonia walked around in a circle, her already too short dress rising even higher as she did. Sonia may be dressed entirely too provocatively, but she still had her looks. Too bad her interior didn't match her exterior.

"You see, I happen to have information regarding someone you work with," Sonia continued. "Someone who you've treated better over the years than your own mother."

Oh, no, she's talking about me. A quick look at Jaleen proved he was thinking the same thing.

"Someone who has been withholding the truth from you and pretending to be someone they're not. Someone who you may or may not be related to."

"As of right now, it only seems like you're talking about yourself," Summer said.

"Oh, but I'm not, Summer. The person I'm talking about could never be me."

Thank God for that.

Jaleen nudged her. "Maybe you should say something before she does," he whispered.

"How?" she whispered back.

Jaleen held her gaze. "Just say what's in your heart, like we practiced."

"The person I'm talking about has spent the last few years tricking all three of you into believing she is something that she isn't." Sonia's voice got even louder. "You see, I never pretend to be anything I'm not. What you see is what you get. But this devious woman? Well, she's the type you need to watch out for. The type who'll pretend to be someone she isn't just to get ahead. And you—" Sonia pointed at Winter, Autumn and Summer, her laugh spiteful. "You fools fell right into her trap."

Sonia took two steps closer to Winter.

Taheim went to step in but Winter put her hand out to stop him. Danni knew what she was doing. She was trying to hold her ground, refusing to back down to Sonia.

"But don't worry," Sonia said, her voice dropping even lower as she reached for Winter's face. "Mama's here to make it all better."

I can't stand this woman. Danni was fuming so much she hadn't noticed she'd completely stepped out of her hiding spot.

"Don't you dare touch me," Winter said, grabbing Sonia by the wrist. "Ever."

Sonia laughed as she turned to look over her shoulder. It took Danni a few seconds to realize she was looking at her.

"So now you want to come out and play," Sonia said, yanking her wrist out of Winter's hand. "I saw you hiding in the back. Do you want to take over from here or should I just keep going?" Sonia waved an arm toward Winter, Autumn and Summer who were each shooting Danni looks of confusion.

Just say it, Danni. Before Sonia goes any further.

Danni walked toward them. "No matter what happens today, please know that I really do love each of you and I am so sorry for everything I've done."

"Oh, please," Sonia muttered under her breath.

"What are you talking about?" Summer asked in concern.

Spit it out, Danni. Spit it out now.

"I'm your half sister," she finally said. "Which means... Sonia is my birth mother." *There, I said it.*

She should feel a big source of relief now that she'd finally said the words out loud to the people she'd feared would learn the truth. Unfortunately, judging by the looks of shock, anger and disbelief written on their faces, she had a feeling her relief would be short-lived.

Chapter 16

Autumn was the first to speak. "How long have you known?"

Danni took a deep breath. "Five years ago. Right before my father passed away, he told me the truth. When I saw the opening for the store manager position at Bare Sophistication, I came here hoping I would get the chance to meet you ladies. I'd gone my entire life believing that my mom was my actual birth mother, only to realize that she wasn't. I was too curious to pass up the opportunity to connect with blood relatives, so I hopped on a plane and uprooted my life to Chicago."

"So you came here knowing this information?" Winter asked, tears brimming her eyes. "Why didn't you say anything?"

"During my interview, I was just trying to get a feel for your personalities. When you called and told me I got the job, I'd planned on saying something after a week or two, but I couldn't…"

"Why?" Autumn asked. "Why would you lie to us for so long and think it was okay?"

"I never thought it was okay," Danni said, her emotions rising. "I knew what I was doing was wrong, but every time I got the courage to tell you all the truth, I got cold feet."

"Is this what you were trying to tell us in the studio earlier?" Winter asked.

"Yes. I was trying to avoid a situation like this."

"Yeah, well, you had plenty of opportunities to avoid something like this happening," Autumn said, crossing her arms over her chest. "Over three years of opportunities to be exact."

"We let you into our lives," Winter said as a couple of tears escaped. "Treated you as if you were family. You had so many chances to be honest."

I am family... Danni stole a glimpse at Sonia. *Don't cry. Don't cry.* Sonia wanted her to cry. She wanted to tell her that she'd told her it would go this way. Crying would only make the situation worse, but when Danni touched her cheek, she realized she was already crying.

Summer hadn't said anything and the hurt look in her eyes broke Danni's heart. "Summer, say something."

"What do you want me to say?" Her voice was void of emotion.

She's not even looking at me. She's looking through me. "What are you thinking? How are you feeling? I can handle it." She honestly wasn't sure if she could handle it, but a yelling Summer was better than a quiet one.

"What am I thinking? Feeling?" Summer took a step closer to her. "Trust me, Danni. You don't want to know what I think about you right now. We see each other almost every day. We both started new lives in Miami together. We lived together before I married Aiden. You may have worked with Winter and Autumn first here in Chicago, but you and me?" Summer's voice slightly broke then. "We were closer."

"I know we were," Danni said. She wanted to reach out to her but thought better of it. "We still are. That doesn't have to change."

Summer briefly closed her eyes. "We're thirteen months apart, right?"

Danni nodded her head. "Yes."

Summer looked at Sonia. "So you gave birth to me, then left and got pregnant with another man's child?"

"Let's not act like you didn't know I was cheating on your father. Danni was a mistake that I just happened to keep. And for what?" Sonia said, looking around. "What good did it do me? You still haven't offered me what I came here for."

"You already delivered the news you came here for," Winter said. "What more could you possibly want?"

"You already know what I want. Look around," Sonia said as she did a 360-degree turn. "Because of me, y'all are a success."

"You don't have anything to do with our success," Autumn said.

"Yes, I do." Sonia placed her hands on her hips. "If it weren't for me knocking you spoiled brats off your high horses so that you could see what the real world was like, you never would have made it out of that small New Jersey town. Your father never had a backbone. Y'all needed tough love and that's exactly what you got from me."

"Tough love?" Winter said, raising her voice. "That's what you call the way you treated us? The way you mentally abused us? The way you wore us down any chance you got, going out of your way to make us feel like it was our fault that you were a terrible mother?"

"Listen here," Sonia said as she pointed her finger at Winter. "The world doesn't give a shit about you. Life isn't wrapped in one pretty red bow and given to you on a silver platter. You have to take what's yours and make the most of the cards you've been dealt. Love is for suckers." Sonia stood straight and smoothed out her dress. "The best thing I could have done for you girls was treat you the way that I did. It made you strong women. Determined women."

Sonia strutted around the room and glanced at the men. "It gave you all this. Successful, good-looking men with money to buy you everything you've ever wanted."

Sonia set her sights on Danni. "Now that I see what my real daughters have made of themselves, I won't need your money anymore."

Real daughters... It shouldn't have hurt, but it did.

"You've been giving her money?" Autumn asked. "Why?"

Danni opened her mouth to speak but Sonia beat her to it. "To pay me for my silence. Duh. She showed up in Vegas sad and lonely, whining about how she believed I was her birth mother and blah, blah, blah. I knew she was telling the truth because she looked just like her daddy. Unfortunately she didn't get any of my features."

Sonia looked Danni up and down as if it left a bad taste in her mouth. "Anyway, I sent her on her way. Until I realized that she'd tracked you all down and was working for you. I knew she didn't have the guts to tell you the truth, so I made her an offer she couldn't refuse."

Danni looked at Autumn first. "She told me that she wouldn't tell you guys my true identity if I paid her." She was so wrapped up in her own emotions that she hadn't noticed Jaleen come to stand near her until she followed Winter's, Autumn's and Summer's eyes. She wasn't surprised when Taheim, Ajay and Aiden went to stand by Winter's, Autumn's and Summer's sides, as well. All eyes were on them. She didn't miss the look of disappointment they were giving Jaleen, either.

"It's okay," he whispered. "I can handle them."

"Aw, isn't this sweet," Sonia said, clasping her hands together. "So who's writing me my next check?"

"We're not giving you any money," Autumn said. "So you can leave now."

Sonia's laugh was filled with disdain. "Oh, really? Well, I wonder what the tabloids will think about this little story. I can picture it now." Sonia raised her hands in the air. "The bastard daughter of Vegas headliner Sonia Dupree has been secretly working for Dupree's daughters in the guise of a lingerie boutique store manager."

Sonia smiled. "Do you know how much publicity I could get from that? Those tabloids love a good story. Face it, you each have something to lose."

Sonia looked at the women. "Aiden, you're some type of famous photographer now, right? And you just opened up a business right down from Summer's new store in Miami. Autumn, didn't you and Ajay just purchase several additional bars and lounges in the Midwest? You were in the paper for that, right?"

Sonia looked from Winter to Taheim. "Didn't you both just create an online clothing app not too long ago? And aren't you set to go on a clothing tour again this fall?"

Sonia glanced around the room. "You see, I have nothing to lose and everything to gain."

"We aren't falling for your BS," Autumn said. "And I think we've already listened to you long enough. You need to leave."

Sonia's smile dropped, then she turned to Danni. "Danni, what about everything I've done for you? You owe me."

"I don't owe you anything." Danni looked at her square in the eye. "And the only thing you've ever given me is a DNA test. Even that I had to beg for. Without it, I wouldn't know for sure that these amazing women are my sisters. But let's get one thing straight, Sonia. That's the only thing you've ever given me."

"Not true, little girl," Sonia said, waving her finger in the air. "Life! I gave you life." Sonia turned to face her other daughters. "I gave all of you life and let's not forget that I could have had each of you sucked from my body the minute I found out I was pregnant. So the next time you decide to team up against me, just remember… I brought you into the world and I can damn sure take you out of it."

With that, Sonia left the shop, leaving a mountain of mess in her wake. Winter, Autumn and Summer looked emotionally and mentally drained.

And it's all my fault.

"I know you ladies don't believe me," Danni said. "But I truly am sorry. I know there is nothing I can say or do that will make this better, but I hope that, in time, you'll want to talk about it."

"There's something you can do for me," Summer said sternly. "Rip up that partner agreement and be out of my condo by the end of the week."

Danni cringed. "Okay, I can do that." *It's the least I can do.*

"Let's give your sisters some time to talk to each other," Jaleen said, wrapping a supportive arm around her.

She looked at each woman one last time, hoping for any sign that she hadn't screwed up as much as she thought she had. That she hadn't just lost some of the most important people in her life. But she didn't see anything other than anger and hurt.

Jaleen held her an entire block before she finally couldn't walk anymore. She felt herself slowly falling to the ground, oblivious to the people walking up and down the busy Chicago street trying to avoid stepping on her.

She barely recalled Jaleen swooping her into his arms and carrying her into an alley. "It's okay. I've got you." His consoling words enveloped her in a blanket of comfort as he set her down. The gravel pavement was rough on her skin and, in a way, she welcomed the pain. She already hurt so much that sitting on sharp gravel that probably contained shards of glass seemed minimal compared to what she'd just experienced.

"I can't believe that just happened," she said in a voice she barely recognized. "That couldn't have gone any worse." Her tears were freely flowing now, creating moist puddles on her shirt and Jaleen's.

Danni couldn't remember the last time she'd cried this hard. The last time she'd felt so much emotion that it almost seemed unbearable. *When Dad passed away*, she thought. *That's the last time I felt like this.* And even then, she'd had two years to prepare for his death.

"I love them so much," she said into Jaleen's chest. "I can't lose them like this."

"Just give them time," Jaleen said. "A lot was thrown at them today. They just need time to process everything."

She heard what he was saying, but deep in her heart she knew that things would never be the same between them. They'd trusted her with so much and, in turn, she'd been lying to them.

As she sat in the alley, clinging to Jaleen with the little energy she had left, she understood all too well what it had taken her years to realize. A part of her had already loved Winter, Autumn and Summer when they met because she'd known they were her birth sisters. After one meeting, she'd realized they were amazing women and were nothing like

Sonia. However, they'd loved her like a sister regardless of a DNA test. They hadn't even known her true identity and they'd loved her anyway. Offered her a part of their business despite the fact that she wasn't blood to them.

That's because you were sisters in all the ways that mattered.

Now she may have lost them forever.

Jaleen checked his watch for the third time in the last ten minutes as he tried to calm his nerves. These past ten days had been extremely difficult. Not only had there been numerous issues with one of the South Beach hotels, but he'd also had to deal with Cordelia popping up in his personal space every chance she got. Luckily, Cordelia was gone and he could finally see the possibility that they would finish the renovations only slightly behind schedule.

"Hey, man," Jesse said as he peeked his head through the door. "Do you need anything before I leave?"

"No, I should have everything under control. I'll lock up soon." Everyone on the job site had already gone for the day. The week hadn't been easy for his contractors, either, but his biggest worry was that Danni wasn't as okay as she seemed.

Every time he'd seen her lately she'd been bubbly and joking around about having free time now that she was out of work. Despite his best efforts to try to convince her to move in with him until she figured something out, she'd insisted she stay in a hotel for a little while instead. He hadn't wanted to argue with her or to make her upset, but he felt like he was growing even more gray hairs worrying about her when they weren't together.

Even though she'd been putting on a good facade, he was elated when she'd agreed to go on their fourth date tonight. He'd been prepared for her to say she didn't want to go, but, thankfully, she'd said it was exactly what she needed.

After everything that had happened, Jaleen had to face the fact that he cared about Danni more than he'd ever cared about any woman before. Which meant he had to have a conversation with his father before he took his relationship with Danni any further.

His phone rang, disrupting his thoughts. "This is Jaleen," he said without looking at the caller ID.

"Hey, man," Taheim said on the other end. "Got a minute?"

Jaleen sighed. "Yeah, I have a few minutes. What's up?"

"You really don't want to talk to me, do you?"

"It's not that," Jaleen said. "JW is supposed to be in Miami today and he agreed to meet me at my office. But he's ten minutes late and not answering my calls."

"Oh, I see."

No, I doubt you really see. "Look, man, I know I missed your calls a couple times this week, but if you're calling to talk about Danni and ask why she didn't tell the women the truth, then I'm not having that conversation with you. Winter may be your wife, but it was hard enough on Danni having that conversation with Sonia there, knowing that she was in a lose-lose situation."

"Wow, that's not what I called for," Taheim said. "Listen, I'm not going to pretend to understand why Danni took so long to tell them, but that's between Winter, Autumn, Summer and Danni. To be honest, I'm glad she has you to lean on."

Jaleen loosened his grip on the phone. "Thanks, man, that means a lot."

"No problem." Both men were silent for a while. "Look, I've never gotten into your family business, but after seeing you and Danni together before everything went down, I had to call and tell you that I think you need to stand up to JW."

Jaleen smiled. "Funny you should say that, because that's exactly why I wanted to meet with him tonight. It might not change anything, but he needs to know how I feel about Danni."

"You already know he's not going to understand, so I hope you have a better plan."

"Yeah, I do." Jaleen thought about everything he'd be giving up if he went through with his plan. "If he can't understand where I'm coming from, then he'll lose me."

"You'd quit?" Taheim asked.

"For Danni? In a heartbeat."

His father had ruled his life for entirely too long and it was past time he did something about it. If his father thought he could continue to rule his life, he had another think coming. There was nothing and no one who would keep him from the woman he loved.

Love? Damn, I love her.

Maybe he'd always known he loved her. He'd always treated her differently. Argued with her any chance he got. He'd even concocted this bet to try to get closer to her, so it was obvious that his mind knew what his heart had just figured out.

"Welcome to the club," Taheim said, breaking his thoughts.

"What did you say?"

"Nothing, man," Taheim said with a laugh. "Seriously, though, I know I don't need to tell you, but Danni's been through a lot and she probably feels as if her world is falling apart right now. Be the reason her world feels like it's finally coming back together, and not the reason it feels more broken. In other words, just make sure you figure everything out before you lose her."

"I will," Jaleen said. "I will."

Unfortunately the first part of his plan would have to wait. He read the incoming text on his phone.

Canceling on me? Again?

It was the second time he'd tried to meet with his father in a week so, clearly, JW wasn't making him a priority.

Chapter 17

Although Danni had been trying to pretend her life wasn't in shambles, she truly appreciated the fact that Jaleen had asked her to go on their fourth date. The only problem with them going on a fourth date was that a fifth date was right around the corner and she didn't know if he'd be interested in still dating past the fifth date.

When Danni had spoken with her mom earlier and finally told her that the Dupree sisters knew the truth, her mom had felt relieved. Regina Allison was even more of a worrier than Danni, so she hadn't been surprised to learn that her mom had spent the past few years hoping that things wouldn't escalate negatively. Once Danni had learned about her mother's fears, she hadn't had the heart to tell her the entire story, nor had she told her about Sonia Dupree. Danni simply stated that the women needed more time to process the information which she guessed was true to some extent.

Aaliyah and Nicole had checked on her, as well. When they'd asked Summer what had happened, Summer had told them she hadn't wanted to talk about it. To Danni, that was worse than her telling them what had happened. Not saying anything meant the wound was still too deep for her.

Danni had decided to tell them what had happened and both women had been beyond surprised. Thankfully they had offered their support and promised to keep an eye on Summer, too. They hadn't said anything out loud, but Danni had noticed the look they'd shared. The four of them had gotten even closer over the past year and the business was doing great. Danni and Summer being at odds meant the dream the four of them had seen for Bare Sophistication Miami no longer looked the way they'd imagined.

Danni glanced in the elongated mirror at her outfit and hair. Tonight she'd chosen to wear an olive A-line dress, cream colored heels and a light sweater in case she got chilly. Her hair was wild and wavy in her natural curls and she had on just enough makeup to accentuate her look. Her mood had been up and down so much lately that her dusty-rose lip gloss was the perfect blend of dark and sassy.

The knock on the door let her know that Jaleen had arrived. The minute her eyes landed on his, she immediately felt better than she had all day. *That's what Jaleen does to me*, she thought. *Even on the bad days, he makes everything better.* He'd chosen to wear dark jeans, a French-blue colored top and blue-and-white Nike gym shoes. It didn't matter if Jaleen was dressed to the nines in a suit or adorned in casual everyday clothes, the man looked sexy in everything he wore.

She welcomed his arms when they wrapped around her body.

"I missed you," he said, staring into her eyes. "How have you been today?"

She rubbed her hands up and down his muscular arms. "Better now that you're here." His lips were on hers before she barely got out the last word. As were most of his kisses, his taste was intoxicating and overwhelming in the best way possible. When he kissed her like that, she could almost forget about all the sadness she'd been filled with lately.

"Are you ready?"

"Yes, let me just grab my bag."

When he'd asked her to pack an overnight bag, she hadn't hesitated. They needed a night together. She needed to get lost in the only thing that could be described as the Jaleen Walker experience.

"No blindfolds this time?" she asked, sitting in his car.

"I have the same blindfold from our last date in my trunk if you want me to get it out," he teased.

Halfway into the ten-minute drive, she'd guessed where he was taking her.

"I hope you're not disappointed," Jaleen said as he led her into his penthouse. Danni walked down the hall and followed the music she heard coming from the living room. His balcony doors were open and there was a tray with a bottle of wine and two glasses, cheese and grapes. The tray was sitting on a large blanket with two square pillows in the center.

"I forgot that Music Under the Stars was going to be taking place across the street," Danni said when they stepped onto the balcony. She tried not to think about the fact that just last week she was living one building over. "It's supposed to be one of Miami's most popular date-night destinations."

"I heard that, too," Jaleen said, coming to stand closer to her. "And I couldn't imagine a more relaxing night than listening to neo soul music underneath the stars…with you."

Her cheeks heated at his statement. Jaleen had always been a sweet-talker, but ever since the situation with her sisters, he'd been even more of a charmer than usual. *How am I going to say goodbye to him if he wants to end this?*

The question had been looping in her mind even before the situation with Sonia and her sisters.

Jaleen hadn't just been a good friend to her since they'd started going on dates. He'd been her rock. Her support system. The one person she couldn't wait to see whenever she needed a pick-me-up. After being forced to put distance between her and her sisters, how was she supposed to let Jaleen go, too?

"Are you okay if we stay in tonight?" he asked.

She glanced at the romantic setting, looking at the two candles that were lit on the table, right before she stepped outside to the balcony.

"It's perfect." *Every moment with you is perfect.*

"You're in the highest balcony in the area."

Danni looked over the balcony at all the people in attendance. It had to be hundreds of couples littered around the area, but she was glad she was with Jaleen, away from the crowd.

"Yes, I am." She glanced over her shoulder just in time to catch the naughty smirk that crossed his face.

They got settled on their comfy pillows and blanket right before the music started. Danni closed her eyes as the opening guitar chords mingled with the piano keys of the first neo soul song of the night. She wasn't sure why, but the melody hit her harder than she'd expected and within minutes she was thoroughly wrapped up in the song. Lyrics soon followed that didn't leave to question that the song wasn't one that had a happy ending. It was filled with heartbreak. Disappointment. Missed opportunity. She didn't open her eyes until the end.

"You were mesmerizing," Jaleen said as he passed her a glass of wine.

She took a sip of her wine. "I wasn't doing anything."

"Yes, you were." He moved closer to her. "You were enjoying the moment. I mean, truly enjoying the moment."

He didn't need to expand on what he meant. All week, she'd been acting overly happy, trying to compensate for the fact that she was nowhere near that. Clearly, her acting skills needed work.

"How has everything been going at work?" she asked.

"Frustrating," he said, taking a sip of his wine. "I think the renovations are finally going to go smoothly from here on, but I've been trying to have an important conversation with my father and I haven't been able to because he's been avoiding me."

"Maybe he's been tied up with work," Danni said.

"No, he's definitely avoiding me because he doesn't want to hear what I have to say. I think he has an idea of what I want to talk about."

She placed her hand on his shoulder. "Is it anything you want to talk to me about? Maybe I could help."

An emotion she couldn't quite place crossed his face. He reached out and touched her hand. "There are so many things I wish I could talk to you about, but I wouldn't even know where to start."

She smiled. "How about the beginning?"

He smiled back at her, but his didn't reach his eyes.

What if he wants to talk to you about the five date rule? What if this was his way of ending what they started?

"Are you trying to find a way to tell me that you don't want to keep dating after our fifth date?" She hoped like hell that wasn't the case, but if it was, she had to be prepared.

"What? No," he said, squeezing her hand tighter. "If anything, I don't want to put a limit to how many dates we go on. I don't want to stop dating you at all." He gazed into her eyes. "Can't you tell by now that I'm crazy about you? That you're the most amazing woman I've ever met?"

His words warmed her heart. "Jaleen, you just helped me—and are still helping me—through one of the craziest times of my life. The amount of support you've selflessly given me has been more than I could ever repay you for."

"I'd do anything for you." His eyes briefly dipped to her lips. "You have to know that already."

"I do know that," she said, lightly touching his cheek. "So you should understand that I'd do anything for you, too."

"I know," he said. "I know you would."

"Then why don't you let me help you?"

A battle of emotions crossed his face, but the most prominent one was secrecy. After everything they'd been through, he was still holding something back and, by the look of it, it was a way bigger issue than she'd originally thought.

He had a few additional stress lines that hadn't been there last week. On the one hand, she knew she could have been the cause of one or two, but she had a feeling that the problem he didn't want to tell her about was the real cause.

Danni thought back to that day they'd been in her condo. The day she'd told him about a few items on her list and the response she'd gotten when she told him that she trusted him. *Don't put too much trust in me, Danni.* He'd meant the words then and, until now, she hadn't really thought about them. How was she not supposed to trust him when he did so many things that were worth her trust?

When Jaleen had originally made the bet, she'd accepted, knowing that their relationship would take a physical turn but never imagining that her heart would be as invested as it already was.

Yes, you did, her inner voice teased. *You knew how you*

felt about Jaleen before you even accepted the terms of the bet.

It was true, he'd always had part of her heart. Guaranteed, it had been the part of her heart she'd reserved solely for those who annoyed her to no end, but still, it had been his.

But now he has your complete heart. Now, he had more of her heart than he'd ever had before. More than he'd ever asked for and more than she'd been willing to give.

But I gave it to him anyway. She'd given him a part of her that she'd sworn she would never give unless she knew the other person was as invested in their relationship as she was. Sitting there, looking into Jaleen's dark brown eyes, she knew it was too late for her to take back what she'd given so freely.

Was he crazy about her? Yes. Did he think she was amazing? Yes. Did that mean she was any less confused about where they stood? No. He may not know how he felt about her. May not share the same strong feelings. But it didn't matter. *I'm in love with him. Deeply, passionately, irrevocably in love.*

He clenched his jaw in the way that he did when there was so much he wanted to say but couldn't. Or wouldn't. *Can he tell what I'm feeling? What I'm thinking?* It was so amazing to her that although many things had changed between them—in a way—a lot was still the same. They still "vibed" off one another's energy. They could still talk to each other without saying many words. Still notice when the other was uncomfortable.

Danni felt broken, tired, confused about where her life was headed and what steps she should take next to fix her circumstances. Looking at Jaleen, observing his behavior, it was clear that he was dealing with the same inner struggles. However, she saw something else when she looked at him, too. She saw a man that, despite what he may be going through, wanted to love her. Wanted to give his heart to her.

Which begged her to ask herself what was standing in his way? And since he wasn't going to tell her how she could help him through this, what was she going to do while he worked it out on his own? The answer was obvious and she was overwhelmed with a clarity she hadn't had in a long time. She'd do what she'd been doing ever since she'd realized she was falling hard for him. She'd love him. And when the moment came when he was ready to talk to her about what was holding him back, she'd listen.

Danni wasn't sure who made the first move, but their lips danced together in an intense lip-lock that had her entire body shaking in need.

Their kiss was filled with unrequited emotion and feelings they hadn't yet discussed. Danni poured years' worth of secrets into that kiss. Months of anxiety over what she should do about her issues and weeks of sadness over the turn her life had taken.

She kissed Jaleen with all she had. His kisses were like her lifeline and were filled with so much passion, it almost brought tears to her eyes.

Her fingers touched the edge of his shirt and lifted it over his head. She went to his jeans next, unbuttoning and unzipping them before easing them down his muscular thighs.

The night wind caught hold of the bottom of her dress as she assisted Jaleen as he removed it with ease. One of his hands played in her hair while the other unsnapped her bra. Danni softly placed her hand on the inside of his boxers, rubbing up and down his shaft before pushing them completely off. The way he grabbed her breasts and sucked her nipples was more erotic than he'd ever been before.

When they'd had sex the previous times, their lovemaking had been patient, exploratory, yet gentle. Hungry yet in no rush to be fulfilled. They'd known it wouldn't be the last time they'd made love. But tonight? Tonight there wasn't anything patient about what they were doing.

Their movements were almost desperate as they worked together to remove her panties. Their kisses harder. Touches bolder. Had Jaleen been a less-prepared man, she wasn't even sure they would have stopped to protect themselves. Honestly, she couldn't have cared at this point. All she could do was feel and live in the moment.

As frantic as they'd been, he entered her slow...smooth. The change of pace caused her to moan loudly into the night air, not caring if she was waking up his neighbors. There wasn't much she cared about right then...except relishing in the feeling of fulfillment she received with Jaleen buried deep inside her.

If any nosy neighbors were watching the act unfold, he was sure he looked like a man possessed as he threw back his head and howled into the sky.

He was pouring his entire soul into their lovemaking and he knew Danni was doing the exact same thing. He could feel it in the way she kissed him, in the way she stroked him, in the way she gazed into his eyes as if he was the answer to her present and future.

As non-poetic as it was, the only word he could think of to describe the feeling coursing through his body was jealousy. He was jealous of all the men in the world who loved a woman like he loved Danni but had no problems expressing their feelings. He was jealous of the couples who could love freely without having to experience the drama and heartache that he and Danni had faced and would still face when he finally had to tell her to truth. He was jealous of who he was three years ago. The Jaleen who had met

Danni and had had more time with her than he had now. That Jaleen was a dumbass because he'd spent years not loving her. Not knowing that she was the woman who'd make him feel emotions he'd never felt before and, the entire time, she'd been right there all along.

He'd stayed away because he'd known she was the one for him. He'd known she would be the one woman he couldn't let go. Even so, knowing it didn't make him any less pissed at his former self.

Losing her was not an option. Not when he'd convinced himself that a woman like Danni didn't exist for him.

He leaned down to kiss her, needing to feel her lips on his. He was selfish. And even knowing that he was being selfish didn't stop him from wanting more of her…in every capacity. He'd made that bet with her knowing that it wasn't fair since she didn't know his whole story. Then when he'd realized he was falling for her, he still couldn't let her go.

"I'm close," Danni said, rotating her hips to meet him stroke for stroke. The rotation combined with her tongue placing kisses across his chest…his arms. Any place she could kiss was his undoing.

Danni shuddered, quivering with need as she exploded in a passionate release.

Jaleen felt his entire body jerk right after hers, tossing his head back and forth at the magnitude of every emotion he'd ever felt ricocheting through his body at one time. He collapsed at Danni's side, pulling her over on top of him.

She lay on his chest, panting as much as he was. Words weren't spoken. Words weren't needed. Some things one could only experience… Loving Danni was one of those things for Jaleen.

Chapter 18

Danni awoke sore and achy in places she never had before. Not that she was complaining. Last night with Jaleen had been one of the best nights of her life and exactly what she'd needed. It had been indescribable. The only thing better than spending an entire night making love to Jaleen was waking up next to him in the morning.

"Hey, beautiful," he said in a gruff voice.

"Good morning." She rubbed her hand against his five-o'clock shadow. "Did you sleep well?"

"Amazing," he said, pulling her to him. His stomach growled. "Maybe I slept a little too well because I brought dinner, but we never got around to eating it."

"And whose fault was that?" she said, playfully hitting his chest.

"How about I warm up the food while you stay here in bed?"

"Sounds like a plan to me."

Danni admired Jaleen's naked body leaving the room before easing back into the covers. *I could get used to this*, she thought as her eyes drifted closed. She was almost back to dreamland when the constant chimes on Jaleen's phone kept going off, indicating he had messages or emails. She tried to ignore it, but she couldn't.

Danni picked up his phone to turn it off but the name across the screen caught her eye.

Cordelia? Why is the appraiser sending so many messages this early in the morning? While she was staring at the phone, Cordelia sent two images back-to-back.

Don't look at it, Danni. It's Jaleen's private phone. She was just about to turn away when the third image caught her eye. She didn't even have to open the image to see what it was. It was a picture of Cordelia and Jaleen together in a pose that didn't look like two old friends at all. They looked more like a couple. Danni hated to seem suspicious, but it also looked pretty recent.

Now I know something's up, she thought when another picture came through that appeared to have been taken the same day. In this picture, Cordelia was sitting on Jaleen's lap and his arms were wrapped around her waist.

"The food has arrived," Jaleen said as he walked in with a tray of what was supposed to have been dinner. Danni pretended as though she'd been stretching and not looking at his phone. She was no longer hungry. Her mind was occupied by the picture on his phone, but she didn't want to ask him and make it seem like she didn't trust him.

"Are you okay?" he asked. "You look as though you've seen a ghost."

Nope. Just a bunch of ruffles wrapped around my man. "No, I'm fine."

Jaleen observed her a few seconds more before walking to his side of the bed. His phone dinged another time and then another. He finally picked it up.

Danni watched Jaleen read through the messages, noticing for the first time that he wasn't able to hold his poker face as well as he usually did.

"Did you look at my phone?" he asked.

Danni shrugged. "I glanced at it because it kept going off."

"What did you see?"

Danni took a bite of the rice that was in the bowl nearest her. She was nervous, although she had no reason to be. He was the one who had to explain the picture. "I only saw two pictures of you and Cordelia together."

"Oh…"

Oh? That's it?

"Jay, why is your appraiser sending you pictures that the two of you took? Better yet, why do you look so cozy in the pictures?"

Jaleen didn't say anything. He just sat there, staring at her.

"Never mind," Danni said. "It's not my business." In some ways she felt like it was. Yet in other ways she felt like it wasn't.

"No, I need to explain," Jaleen said. "I've put off telling you long enough and you have a right to know why I was so hot and cold when Cordelia arrived."

Jaleen turned to face her and, by instinct, Danni pulled the sheet higher on her body as a protective shield.

"Cordelia's family is very close with my family and the way our families operate is somewhat unconventional."

Oh, no. Please tell me this isn't a weird fetish thing. Danni had once dated a man she'd later found out loved to be with his dog a little too much. The entire situation disgusted her. She almost swore off relationships that day.

If she'd overcome the confession her ex had made when he informed her that he'd fallen in love with his dog, there was no way she couldn't handle what Jaleen had to tell her, right?

"Twenty years ago, our parents made an agreement," Jaleen said.

Danni squinted in confusion. "What kind of agreement?"

"A marriage agreement of convenience," he said, maintaining eye contact.

Oh, crap, he's serious.

"Your parents arranged for you and Cordelia to be married? Does that mean you're engaged?"

"Technically, yes. But I never proposed. It was never that type of arrangement. They've discussed our future marriage since I was fifteen years old, but not in the traditional sense."

"Are you kidding me!" she yelled, standing from the bed, not caring that she was naked. "You've been engaged this entire time? You've been cheating on your fiancée this entire time?"

"It's not like that," Jaleen said, standing beside her. "Our fathers made a business arrangement. I got my arrangement pushed back until my thirty-fifth birthday. Therefore, we aren't officially engaged until then."

"Oh, you're right," Danni said sarcastically. "You'll be thirty-five soon, but who cares, right?"

Jaleen stepped closer to her. "That's not what I mean," he said in a calming voice. "There is no way I'm marrying Cordelia. The only reason I took those photos was to make her father happy. I may be going through hell with mine, but Cordelia is close to her father."

Danni shook her head, unable to comprehend the fact that Jaleen was soon-to-be engaged. "Do you love her?"

"Of course not."

"But you'd planned to marry her at some point?" She knew how arranged marriages worked, but she hadn't actually met anyone who was already promised to someone else.

"Danni," Jaleen said, lightly touching her shoulders. "I know that this doesn't make sense to you and I'm a complete jerk for waiting so long to tell you. But please know that I do not and will never love Cordelia. And I'm not marrying her. My brothers' marriages were arranged. My parents, aunt and uncle's. My cousin's, as well. So maybe at one point, I was fine with the idea because I was raised with the notion that life was going to be that way. But that's before I met you. That's before I fell for you."

He took her face in his hands. "It's before I knew what being with a woman who I truly cared about felt like."

Danni calmed down…a little. "What happens if you don't marry her? What about the agreement?"

Jaleen cringed. "If I don't marry Cordelia, Walker Realty Partner will lose a lot of money."

"Will it be able to survive the loss?"

"The South Beach renovations could help keep the company surfaced for a while."

"But it couldn't save it, could it?"

She already knew the answer. It was written all over his face. *Nope, this is officially worse than my creepy dog-loving ex.* At least she hadn't been in love with her ex. Jaleen, on the other hand, had just broken her heart and then tried to piece it back together with sticky glue because there was no way she was going to be the cause of him losing everything he'd fought so hard to save.

"I'd give up much more if it meant being with you," he said sweetly. "I never liked the idea of my future already being defined, but back then it felt like I didn't have a choice."

I can relate to that. She'd felt as if she hadn't had a choice when Sonia had given her the ultimatum to pay up or she'd tell her secret. However, despite the fact that she'd felt that way, it hadn't been her only choice. It had only been the choice she'd decided to make at the time.

"You said when you met me you knew you could never marry Cordelia." She searched his eyes. "Is that true?"

Jaleen stepped closer to her. "I know I may not have always acted like it, but, deep down, I'd always known you would be my future… If it was something you wanted, too."

I want that. Oh, man, do I want that. "But we never even dated until recently."

Jaleen shook his head. "Just because we weren't officially dating didn't mean I didn't know what type of woman you were. In all the ways that mattered, we'd dated. We just took our relationship to another level when I moved to Miami, that's all. The foundations for an amazing relationship were already there. We'd been setting the stage for something worth fighting for the day we met at the bar."

Danni sighed. *I really want to believe him.* However, she didn't know how she was supposed to ignore the fact that he was still technically spoken for. The number-one fear she'd had when she'd started this journey with Jaleen was falling hard for him just to turn around and have to give him up. He was telling her everything she wanted to hear, but how could she trust him when he'd been lying for so long?

"You don't believe me, do you? You don't believe that my feelings for you are real?"

"It's not that," she said in a soft voice. "I just feel blindsided and, given what I just put my sisters through, I'm the last one to judge. But hearing there's a possibility that you belong to someone else is hard to wrap my head around." She looked at him, her eyes glistening with unshed tears.

"Can I see the contract?" she asked. "I think I need

to see it to truly understand." She didn't know why she wanted to see the contract that inevitably held her fate in its hands, too, but she needed more details. She needed to try to rationalize everything she'd just learned.

"Jay, I know how much our relationship has grown, but I understand more how my sisters felt when I told them I was their sister than I ever have before." She blinked for a little longer than she'd meant to. "We've shared so much, but there is still so much more that we don't know about each other. You've been saying those words for months and I wasn't listening then…but I'm listening now."

Jaleen observed her through tentative eyes. "I've got something better than the contract," Jaleen said, walking to his closet. He pulled out a leather portfolio from the top shelf and handed it to her.

She read the inscription. "'Diminished dreams and unspoken promises.'" She ran her hands over the deep ridges of the letters. "What's this?"

"It's everything about me," he said, glancing at his portfolio. "The parts of my life that have been good. The parts of my life that have been bad. We've shared so much with one another, but you're right, there is still so much more to share. Maybe this will give you some more insight into me as a man growing up in the type of family I have. Like you said to me one time, I've been the funny guy. The life of the party. I can play the role of Mr. Charming and work a room.

"On the surface, it seems like I have great communication skills. But the truth is, I have a difficult time expressing myself sometimes, so I write things down to get them out. The stuff in that portfolio is some of the things that I have the hardest time articulating. If after you read it, you still don't understand, then I'll explain everything to you to the best of my ability for as many times as you need me to."

Wow, I think I just fell a little harder for this man.
Danni held the book to her chest. "Okay, I'll read it."

If she had asked to take it back to her hotel room so that she could look through the portfolio in privacy, he would have agreed and even driven her there himself. But she hadn't asked to do that. She hadn't even asked him to leave the room.

Danni sat back in the bed and wrapped the sheets around her naked body. She was trembling as she opened the portfolio and knowing that he was the cause made him even more upset with himself than he already was. He sat next to her, covering himself with the other half of the sheet.

She'd taken the news much better than he'd expected, which meant Taheim and Jeremiah had been right all along...he should have just told her the truth from the beginning. *She's still uncertain if I really care enough about her to throw it all away.* He couldn't even blame her for being so unsure about the situation. He'd dropped a bomb on her after she'd already experienced a couple of weeks of heartache. Or more like years of heartache if he thought about the secrets she'd lived with.

"Oh, my goodness," Danni said with wide eyes. "You lost your virginity to someone your dad picked out?"

"Yeah," Jaleen said. "I was fifteen and apparently JW believed that was too old for a Walker man to still be a virgin. I didn't think anything of it when the seventeen-year-old girl from down the street started spending time with me. I'm not going to pretend I didn't enjoy it, but when I found out, I didn't talk to my father for two months."

Danni's eyes saddened. "You were just a kid." She looked back down and flipped another page in the portfolio. After a few minutes she dabbed away a few tears in her eyes.

"Are you reading about my grandfather?"

"Yes," she said, sniffling. "He seems like he was a great man. You've mentioned him before, but it's obvious that you two had a very close relationship. He's the one who taught you how to flip your first property?"

"He did," Jaleen said with a smile. "I guess that's why I love what I do so much. My grandfather was grooming me to take over the business one day and he didn't care that I was his youngest grandchild. We had a bond that couldn't be broken."

"And he was obsessed with names that begin with the letter *J*," Danni said with a laugh as she read the list of names of his family members. "That's too funny. What about your mom? Just a coincidence or did she change her name to purposely start with a *J*?"

"Just a coincidence. Her first name is actually Susan, but she always thought Jocelyn had more flare, so she's always gone by her middle name. The entire *J* thing got so bad our dogs even had *J* names," Jaleen said, joining in her laughter. "My grandfather even let me name all the family pets because I always came up with the best names."

Danni's eyes darkened. "So a part of the reason your father gives you a hard time is because you're so much like your grandfather?"

Jaleen flinched. "If you ever want to get on JW's bad side, remind him of the one person in the world he'd always tried to be just like but couldn't even come close to."

"Your grandfather…was his name Jay?"

"How'd you guess that? I didn't write that in there."

Danni briefly glanced at his lips before meeting his gaze again. "Because I know you and I'm learning to read between the lines." She smiled sweetly.

Jaleen hadn't known how badly he'd been waiting for a smile from her until she blessed him with one.

Ten minutes later Jaleen had witnessed Danni go through a range of emotions. She laughed. Cried. Got angry. Got happy. The portfolio really was a snapshot of his life, all enclosed in the warm confines of a leather binding. *She's almost to the contract.* There was a chance that the contract wouldn't go over as well as he hoped.

Her shoulders tensed when she got to a picture of him and Cordelia as kids. "So you both have known each other for years?"

"Yes, we met when we were kids. Our families are good friends and, as I said before, we were raised with a lot of the same values."

"I didn't know marriages were still arranged for reasons other than religious ones."

"It's not exactly an arranged marriage," Jaleen said. "More like a marriage of convenience for financial, political, social and business reasons, which has always been the case with my family. Marriages between families such as mine and Cordelia's are meant to help both families profit financially and help secure a solid relationship between any businesses those families may own. We're taught that it's one of the strongest bonds a business can make. It all started in the 1930s when family businesses had to band together to try and survive The Great Depression. Over time, it continued and morphed into what it is today.

"My great-grandparents believed in it and it was passed down to their children, their children's children, and so on. Cordelia's grandfather and my grandfather used to be best friends. My grandfather founded his real-estate business while Cordelia's grandfather started a property appraiser's business. So naturally, JW and Cordelia's father became friends, having grown up together. JW took over my grandfather's company and Cordelia's father took over for his father."

Danni glanced from the portfolio to him. "And your father betrayed Cordelia's father?"

"Pretty much. JW and Mr. Rose often invested in some of the same businesses. JW made a bad business deal and the only one who really lost any money was Mr. Rose. Since they had once been close friends, Mr. Rose trusted JW again, only to have his trust betrayed, again."

"And none of that was grounds to break the agreement that you and Cordelia marry?"

I wish. Jaleen ran his hand down his face. "If anything, it only made things worse. You've met Cordelia. She's always been...unique in her own way. She's a good person but, like I said, our families share the same values and despite the fact that JW has wronged her father one too many times, her father is a businessman. JW owes him and he owes him big. A marriage between the Rose and Walker family would also mean JW would receive a silent investment from Mr. Rose in a hefty lump sum of money."

"So to both your fathers, you and Cordelia are just..."

"A business deal," Jaleen said, finishing her statement. "A marriage of convenience to keep it all in the family. It's almost like Cordelia's father and JW know how ruthless the other is, so you keep your friends close but your enemies closer."

Danni closed the portfolio, anger evident in her eyes. It didn't seem directed at him, though. It was anger over the situation. "Were you going to marry her for your father? Your family? Or your grandfather's legacy?"

"My grandfather's legacy and my family," he said quickly, until her intuitive look made him reconsider his response.

Who am I doing this for? Jaleen really thought about her question. He definitely wasn't doing it for himself, but his initial response hadn't been completely true, either. "And my father," he finally said. "In some really messed-up way, I guess I didn't want to be the disappointment he always saw me as. Even if I'd done everything wrong in his eyes, I wanted to finally do something right."

Her eyes softened as she placed the portfolio on the bed. "Thank you for sharing this with me." She reached out to clasp his hand. "You already know that I think you are an amazing man. Your portfolio only confirmed what I was already feeling."

I feel a "but" coming. He didn't want to lose her, but the situation was less than ideal.

"But I think I need to spend some time with my mom back in Tampa," Danni finally said. "I believe you when you say that you won't go through with the wedding and don't want to lose me. However, I also know how much Walker Realty Partner means to you and it seems like you still haven't quite figured out how to get out of this dilemma."

Jaleen had an idea of what he was going to do next, but he didn't want to tell Danni until he knew for sure it would work.

"Between what happened with my sisters and learning about you and Cordelia, I think I need to take some time to focus on myself and try to piece my life back together." Danni placed her hand on his cheek. "But that doesn't mean I'm not here if you need me. That's the least I could do after you've been by my side through all my drama."

Damn, she's amazing. Even after an emotional morning she'd never seen coming, she was still offering to be there for him.

"I understand," he said, relieved when she allowed him to pull her into his arms. As unrealistic as it was, he wished he could keep her there forever.

Chapter 19

"Do you understand what your decision will do to the company? What it will do to our reputation?"

Jaleen stayed standing, refusing to sit. "You can't play with your children's lives as if we're pieces on a chessboard," he said, his eyes trained on JW. "It's always about how someone else's decisions will affect the company, but you fail to see the fault in your own actions."

It had taken Jaleen five days to get JW to agree to meet with him. He'd even flown to Chicago to make it as easy as possible. When he'd arrived, he hadn't been surprised to see Jeremiah, Joel and Uncle Jake already in the conference room. Jeremiah had already warned him that JW had invited them to the meeting. His cousin Jasper was even on speed dial.

"Listen to yourself," JW said. "You think I don't know that you've been dating that Danni girl. Remember, I have eyes everywhere. So now you think you're in love and you want to break tradition."

"You don't care about tradition," Jaleen said, keeping his voice even. "You're more concerned with breaking a business deal than anything else. You had two of your sons get married to women they didn't love, and look how those business deals worked out for you. You just lucked out because your sons grew to love their wives and now they couldn't be happier. And even you and Mom, and Uncle and his wife had grown up together, so the circumstances were different."

"You and Cordelia grew up together."

"As friends, not lovers." Jaleen placed his hands on the conference table. "After all the decisions you've forced this family to make, the company is still failing, and unless you change the dirty way you do business, it's only going to get worse. Hell, it already is worse."

"Jaleen's right," Uncle Jake said. "We've all seen the writing on the wall for years. This is not the type of business Dad envisioned."

"Maybe we should reevaluate the business," Jeremiah suggested. "We'd have to make some tough decisions and downsize, but Jaleen has some great ideas about starting over and I think, if you'd just hear him out, you'd agree that it's possible to save the company in the long run."

JW cut his eyes at Jaleen. "Ideas! What? You think you could run this company better than me? No one could run this company better than me. I took Walker Realty Partner to a new level. It was my business sense that made shit happen." JW pounded his chest. "You think I'm the only business owner playing dirty to get ahead? Think again."

Jaleen looked at his father. *Really* looked at him. He'd aged a lot over the years and although he'd still maintained his looks, Jaleen noticed certain features about him that he hadn't noticed before. There was a lot of regret in the stress lines of his forehead and fatigue from probably spending one too many nights trying to take shortcuts in the business rather than doing things the right way. There was also something else in his eyes when you looked past the anger. Something he couldn't quite place. Out of all the times he'd tried to get his father to see reason, he'd never asked him one important question.

"Why are you so angry at the world and so jaded by your life that the only way you can see this business being successful is by becoming the very man you used to warn us not to be?"

For a brief millisecond Jaleen saw vulnerability in the way JW was looking at him. "Are you so blinded by your righteous attitude that you fail to see what I've been trying to get you to see for years?"

Jaleen had no idea what JW was talking about. "And what exactly should I be seeing?"

"You should be seeing that no matter how hard you try you could never be me. You could never take my place."

"I've never wanted to take your place," Jaleen said. "For years I wanted to work beside you to help make this company great. But you were so blinded by your hatred toward me that I never got the chance."

"You're damn right," JW said, his voice growing louder.

Although Jaleen had already known that fact, hearing that his own father truly despised him was a tough pill to swallow.

"Why?" Jaleen asked, finally raising his voice. He stepped closer to JW, invading his personal space. "I'm your son. Your flesh and blood. What the hell did I ever do to you to make you despise me so much?"

"You were born," JW said, his stare cold and unapologetic. "No son of mine would have done to me what you did."

"What did I do besides love you as your child?" Jaleen said. "What did I do?" he repeated when JW didn't speak.

"You loved him more," JW finally said in a stern voice. "You loved my father more than you loved me and because of that, he loved you in a way he should have loved his own sons. Especially his oldest son. You robbed me of a relationship I should have had with my father because by the time that old bastard grew old and actually started giving a damn about his kids, you were the one that got his love. The only one. Not me, his son who'd been busting his ass to prove that he could run his business."

Jaleen took a step back, briefly glancing at his uncle who seemed to already know that was the reason JW had been so difficult on him all these years. He looked at his brothers, noticing that they didn't look too surprised, either. If he was honest with himself, he realized, he should have been the least surprised of them all. *Jealousy*, he thought. *That's the look I couldn't place.*

"All this time, you've treated me so poorly because you've been jealous of the relationship Grandfather and I had?"

JW just stared at him. His eyes still full of anger and his body language proving that, even at his age, he'd throw punches if he needed to.

Suddenly it didn't matter that Jaleen loved the company his grandfather had built and had spent the majority of his life trying to maintain the legacy of the one man he looked up to. It didn't matter that he'd spent years trying to get his father's approval only to realize he'd never get it. It didn't matter that he'd wasted years of his life living in the moment because he knew one sheet of paper and a man with way too much power would define his entire future. There was only one thing left to do and he no longer had a problem making the decision he knew in his heart he had to make.

"I quit," Jaleen said. "I can't do it anymore." With that, he walked out the door for what he hoped would be the last time. He had better things to do than continue to debate a losing argument. There was only one person on his mind he wanted to be with. One woman who'd completely captured his heart and there was no way he was putting off seeing her any longer. She may have needed space, but he needed her...in every way.

Danni sat on the back porch swing, letting the sun beat down on her face. It was a beautiful May day and the birds were chirping away in the birdhouse she'd brought her mother.

"There you are," Regina said as she stepped out onto the porch. "I've been looking for you all over the house. Are you okay?"

Am I okay? She'd asked herself that question several times over the past two weeks and now she could honestly say that she was.

"I'm fine, Mom." Danni had done quite a bit of soul-searching since she'd arrived in Tampa and her mom had been there to support her up-and-down emotional journey the entire time.

"Good, because there's someone here to see you," Regina said, nodding at the back door.

Danni sat up immediately. *Could it be Jaleen?* She'd missed him so much. They'd texted and had long calls, so she knew that he officially wasn't marrying Cordelia, but he hadn't told her any details. He'd respected that she'd needed space. Now all she had to do was to tell him that he was giving her too much space.

Her eyes were trained on the door when it opened. *Oh, my goodness*, she thought. It may not be Jaleen, but it was the next best thing.

Winter, Autumn and Summer stood on the other side of the screen.

"Or I guess I should say, several people are here to see

you," Regina said before going back into the house to give them some privacy.

"Um, hi," Danni said, her mouth suddenly dry. They hadn't talked in over a month, so she had no idea what to say to them. *Should I start with sorry? Or maybe let them talk first?*

"How have you been?" *There, that works.*

"We've been okay," Winter said. "Wondering how you were doing, too."

"We shouldn't have let you leave the boutique like that," Autumn said. "It was wrong of us not to make sure you were okay."

"You don't have to apologize," Danni said. "I was the one who betrayed your trust and lied about my identity. You had every right to be upset."

"That may be true," Winter said, glancing at Autumn and Summer before looking back at Danni. "But when it comes to sisters, even if we're mad or fight with one another, family is family even if they make stupid decisions. We're sorry for taking this long to see it."

Danni laughed nervously. "Do you mean that? That you consider me a sister?"

"Danni, we've always considered you a sister," Winter said. "Otherwise we wouldn't have made you the offer to be partner."

"And invited you into our lives," Autumn added. "We never needed a DNA test to tell us how we felt about you. All we wished was that you had been honest and told us the truth up front."

Danni was overwhelmed with happiness, but there was one person present who had yet to say anything. Danni glanced over at Summer who was looking at her with a look she couldn't decipher. Although she'd missed Winter and Autumn, she'd missed her relationship with Summer the most.

"Are we okay?" Danni asked, stepping closer to Summer. Summer's eyes filled with tears before she surprised Danni by what she said next.

"I need my best friend and Bare Sophistication partner back," Summer said, pulling her into a tight hug. "Miami isn't the same without you and neither is the boutique… or me."

Danni hugged her back just as tightly. "I've missed my best friend, too. More than you'll ever know." Danni stepped back to look at all three of the women.

"I love each of you so much and I am so sorry for what I did."

"We're sorry, too," Autumn and Winter said at the same time.

"And we love you, too," Summer chimed in as the four hugged in a way that let Danni know that everything was going to be okay.

"Oh, wait," Danni said, snapping her fingers. "What about Sonia's threat to go to the tabloids? You think she will do that?"

"Of course she would," Autumn said. "But she hasn't yet, which means she's stalling for something. Probably waiting for one of us to pay her off."

"So we have an idea," Winter said. "We'll offer the exclusive story to a well-known magazine instead. There are a couple we've worked with in the past that we trust."

"Are you willing to do that?" Danni asked, looking at each of the women. "Are you willing to tell the world about me and Sonia?"

"Sweetie, there's nothing to tell," Summer said. "You're our sister and that's that."

Autumn placed her hands on her hips. "And regarding

Sonia, the only thing the article will do is expose what a horrible mother she is. But we don't want her to be the main focus. We're going to focus on our business and sisterhood instead."

Sisterhood... I actually have sisters!

"There's someone else here who's been dying to see you," Summer said, clearing her throat. "Oh, lover boy, you can come out now."

Danni turned in time to see Jaleen coming through the back door. *Oh, I've missed him so much.* She never thought it was possible to miss someone so much. She noticed her mom in the kitchen window looking at her with the biggest smile on her face. *That woman will always be the only mother I'll ever need.* Regina was one of a kind and Danni wouldn't trade her for anything.

"We'll wait for you two inside," Winter said, tugging on Summer's and Autumn's arms.

"Good idea." Autumn looked at Winter. "When you said family is family earlier, you weren't including Sonia Dupree in that, were you?"

Winter shot her a look of disbelief. "Do you even have to ask that?"

"Just making sure," Autumn said. "Because I refuse to believe that awful woman gave birth to us."

Danni laughed as the women filed inside before turning her attention to Jaleen. He looked a little tired, like he'd been through hell and back, but he was still devastatingly handsome. When she sat on the porch swing, he went to sit beside her.

"I've missed you," Jaleen said, intertwining his hand with hers.

"I've missed you, too," Danni said. "I was starting to wonder if you were ever going to come see me."

"I knew when I came here that I had to have a good reason for bringing you back to Miami. So I wanted to tie up a few loose ends first."

"Like what?" Danni asked.

"Like the fact that I quit my job a week ago."

Danni's eyes grew big. "You quit your job?"

"Yeah, it's a long story that I will definitely tell you all about later. And I know I already told you that you didn't have to worry about the situation with Cordelia since that's no longer an issue."

"How did she take it?"

"You've met Cordelia. She cursed me out with a few Southern metaphors," Jaleen said with a laugh. "But in the end, she agreed that we were better off as friends. I honestly don't think she wanted to marry me any more than I wanted to marry her, but she was trying to make her father happy."

"I feel bad for her," Danni said. "It's not easy disappointing a parent."

"It's not," Jaleen agreed. "But it's even worse when you've been working so hard not to disappoint a parent, just to learn it had all been a complete waste of energy."

"JW?"

"The one and only." Jaleen placed a kiss on the back of her hand. "I'd planned on seeing you a week ago right after I quit. But a few hours after I left, my uncle called and told me he'd been investigating my grandfather's will."

"Did he find anything?" Danni asked.

Jaleen was already shaking his head in disbelief. "JW had paid my grandfather's lawyer to forge part of the will. My grandfather had never left him the company. In his original will, he'd stated that JW was to run the company until my thirtieth birthday."

"So your grandfather had left it to you to run?"

"Yes, he'd wanted me to run the business and had even

left a letter stating that he knew I'd take the company in the direction it needed to go."

"And JW found out and took matters into his own hands…" Danni's voice trailed off. "So what does that mean? You didn't quit after all?"

"It means, after we figure everything out, I'm initiating my plan to completely rebrand Walker Partner Realty. I spent the past week in meetings with my lawyers, brothers, uncle and cousin trying to figure out a plan of action as to how we want the information to get to the press and how we will inform the employees."

"So you'll be saving the company," Danni said in excitement. "I'm so proud of you."

"I haven't saved it yet, but I'm confident that I have what it takes to make it happen."

"I know you do," Danni said, briefly kissing his cheek. "When do you get to work?"

"In a few days," Jaleen said, holding her gaze. "I told my uncle that I couldn't start anything until I found the woman I love and told her how much she means to me."

He loves me… Danni was pretty sure her smile was so wide that it looked as if her face was stuck that way. "Oh, really," she said, placing her forehead on his. "That's funny, because I was here in Tampa waiting for the man I love to find me and he just so happened to pick the most beautiful day in May to do so."

When Jaleen pulled her in for a kiss, she poured all her love into it. It was just the beginning of the beautiful journey they were about to embark on…together.

This kiss ended way too soon. "I love you," he said, rubbing his thumb against her cheek. "I've wanted to tell you that for so long."

Her heart swelled. "I love you more," she said, sneaking another quick kiss. "But you know what sucks?"

"What?"

"All the sex we missed out on while we were both unemployed for a week."

"I'm sure Summer won't make you start work right away. And I don't plan on starting for a few more days." Jaleen looked at his watch. "If we leave right now, we can make up for lost time."

"You're crazy." Danni was laughing so hard, her stomach hurt. "I'd have to pack up my stuff and tell my mom I'm going back."

"Can you pack up fast? You have three sisters in there who can help you."

"Let's go inside and ask them."

Danni and Jaleen walked back inside to find her mom showing baby pictures of Danni, her brothers and her father to Winter, Autumn and Summer. The sight nearly brought tears to her eyes. After having to deal with a mother like Sonia, her sisters needed to bond with a mother like Regina.

"I can't leave while they're bonding," Danni whispered.

"I understand, but I have an idea." Jaleen brought his mouth to her ear. "Four blocks down, I saw a house for sale that sits right on the beach."

"Looking for new properties to flip already?" Danni asked.

"No, I'm looking for a place to bring the woman I love so that I don't have to spend the night sharing her with four other people."

"You're insane," Danni said with a laugh. "But I love you for it."

"So does that mean you're in?"

She quirked an eyebrow. "In for what exactly?"

Jaleen glanced at the other women to make sure they

weren't eavesdropping. "I still owe you a fifth and final fantasy date."

"So you want us to trespass on private property for our last date? We could just get a hotel. Besides, I doubt the house is even furnished, so it may not be comfortable."

Jaleen held her gaze. "Full disclosure?"

"Full disclosure."

"I contacted the Realtor of the property and got the keys for the night. I want to check it out as a possible investment."

Danni's eyes widened in surprise. *Lawd, I love this man.*

"It's also fully furnished," Jaleen said. "I packed a cooler containing vegetarian dishes and treats from Artemela Rojas. It's in the trunk of my car. I also packed a big fluffy blanket and two pillows...the same ones from that special night we spent on the balcony. All you have to do is pack an overnight bag."

Her eyes darkened as her heart grew even more for the amazing man staring back at her. She pulled him around the corner into the hallway so that they wouldn't have to continue to talk low. "I can be ready in ten minutes."

A sly smile crossed his face. "That's good to know because after this date is over, I'm thinking we need to participate in another bet before your birthday. I need an excuse to help you fulfill any lingering items on your list."

"Oh," she said, returning his smile. "What are the stakes this time?"

Jaleen nuzzled her neck. "I'm thinking if I win, you have to marry me so that we can spend the rest of our lives together."

She studied his eyes. "And if I win?"

He kissed her then, slow and full of passion, his tongue branding hers in a way that left none of his feelings to question. "If you win…" he finally said. "You have to marry me so that we can spend the rest of our lives together."

Sounds like a win-win to me!

* * * * *

*Faith Alexander's guardian angel has a body built for
sin. Ever since she woke up in the hospital after a car
crash, her rescuer, Brandon Gray, has been by her side—
chivalrous, caring and oh-so-fine. All Brandon's focus is
on his long-coveted role as CEO—until he stops to help
a mysterious beauty. With chemistry this irresistible, he's
ready to share a future with Faith, but he feels beyond
betrayed to discover what she's been hiding. If desire
and trust can overcome pride, he'll realize he's found the
perfect partner in the boardroom and the bedroom...*

Read on for a sneak peek at
GIVING MY ALL TO YOU, the next exciting
installment in author Sheryl Lister's
***THE GRAYS OF LOS ANGELES** series!*

She frowned. *Who in the world...?* As if sensing her scrutiny,
he opened his eyes and pushed up from the chair. Faith blinked.
He was even taller than she originally thought, well-built and
easily the most handsome man she'd seen in a long time.

"Hey," he said softly.

"I thought I dreamed you."

His deep chuckle filled the room. "No. I'm very real."

Faith tried to clear the cobwebs from her mind. "You helped
me when I crashed." She thought for a moment. "Brandon?"

He nodded. "How are you feeling?"

"Everything hurts. Even breathing hurts." She closed her
eyes briefly. "Um...what time is it?" she murmured.

Brandon checked his watch. "A little after eleven."

"You've been here all this time?"

"For the most part. I brought your stuff and I didn't want to leave it with anyone without your permission." He placed them on the tray.

"Thank you."

"Do you want me to call your husband or family?"

Faith wanted to roll her eyes at the husband reference, but just the thought made her ache, so she settled for saying "I'm not married."

"What about family—Mom, Dad?"

The last person she wanted to talk to was her mother. "My parents don't live here," she added softly. She had been on her way to her father's house, but chickened out before arriving and had turned around to go back to the hotel when she'd had the accident.

A frown creased his brow. "You don't have anyone here?"

"No. I live in Oregon. I just got here yesterday."

"Hell of a welcome."

"Tell me about it," she muttered.

"Well, now that I know you're okay, I'm going to leave. I'll stop by to see you tomorrow to make sure you don't need anything." Brandon covered her uninjured hand with his large one and gave it a gentle squeeze.

Despite every inch of her body aching, the warmth of his touch sent an entirely different sensation flowing through her. The intense way he was staring at her made her think he had felt something, as well.

"I…um…" Brandon eased his hand from hers. "Get some rest." However, he didn't move, his interest clear as glass. After another moment he walked to the door, but turned back once more. "Good night."

"Good night." Faith watched as he slipped out the door, her heart still racing. Her life seemed to be a mess right now, but knowing she would see Brandon again made her smile.

Don't miss GIVING MY ALL TO YOU
by Sheryl Lister, available May 2017
wherever Harlequin® Kimani Romance™
books and ebooks are sold.

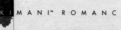

There's no mistaking
the real thing

Bridget Anderson

The Only One for
Me

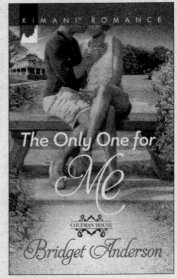

Running the shop at her family's B and B offers Corra Coleman
a fresh start after her unhappy marriage—and a tantalizing
temptation in the form of millionaire Christopher Williams. With
Corra's ex trying to win her back, can Chris show her how love is
supposed to be?

COLEMAN HOUSE

Available April 2017!

HARLEQUIN®

www.Harlequin.com

KPBA495

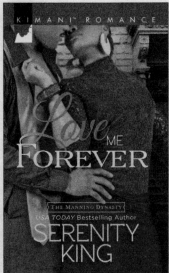